PRETTY DEAD

Also by Francesca Lia Block:

Pretty DEAD

FRANCESCA LIA BLOCK

HARPER TEEN

An Imprint of HarperCollinsPublishers

HarperTeen is an imprint of HarperCollins Publishers.

Pretty Dead
www.harperteen.com

Library of Congress Cataloging-in-Publication Data
Block, Francesca Lia.
    Pretty dead / Francesca Lia Block.—1st ed.
        p.   cm.
    Summary: Beautiful vampire Charlotte finds herself slowly
changing back into a human after the mysterious death of her best
friend.
    ISBN 978-0-06-154785-0
        [1. Vampires—Fiction.   2. Supernatural—Fiction.
3. Death—Fiction.]   I. Title.
PZ7.B61945Pn   2009   2008045068
[Fic]—dc22   CIP
                                                  AC

Typography by Alison Klapthor
09 10 11 12 13   LP/RRDB   10 9 8 7 6 5 4 3 2
❖
First Edition

For T.D. and J.B.
in peace

Acknowledgments

I am grateful to Lydia Wills, Tara Weikum, Jocelyn Davies, Laura Kaplan, Joanna Cotler and everyone at Harper Collins for their work on this book. I had wonderful creative input from Sera Gamble, Tracey Porter and Carmen Staton. None of my books would be possible without the love and support of my friends and family.

Charlotte

Teenage girls are powerful creatures. I remember; I was once one of them. They are relentless and underutilized. They want what they want, and they will do what they must to get it. Love, possessions, beauty, food, sweets, friends. Unless they are crushed so hard as to give up. But then they are just as relentless, only seeking different things. Destruction, annihilation. Unless they can find a way to birth something beautiful out of themselves. In this way teenage girls and Night's children are not that much different, are we?

What William Saw

It's amazing how beautiful destruction can appear. If we don't judge it, don't put value on it, it's just color and light and motion. You can think of it as a kind of art.

The sky is red. Every sunset like a warning of disasters still to come.

She sits by the pool, tiled like the ones we saw in Rome so long ago. She is wearing a big white hat and sunglasses, but I can see she is staring out at the red-tinged sea below the cliffs beyond her house. The movieland villa, the tiny palace bought by someone else, a man, now dead, the one she left me for. But she didn't really leave me for him. She just needed to go. And all these years I've wandered the earth, looking for her. She left no easy trace.

My Charlotte. Mine.

I wonder what she is thinking. I remember how her body felt, the long, lean limbs, the sharp, curved hipbones, the swell of her breasts. I remember the plumpness of her lips and the way her eyelids trembled, her eyes shattered blue glass turned skyward when I pressed my lips to her swan neck.

She doesn't think I am capable of love; perhaps she is right. But what is dreaming of someone for a hundred years? Isn't that a form of love? Isn't love following her across the world and waiting, hidden in the dark, watching her, afraid to approach because of what you might lose? I took something from her once, so long ago. Seeing her now, I wonder why I have followed her all this way, looked for her for so long. She doesn't want to come away with me. How weary she is of this world.

The girl beside her reminds me of Charlotte when we first met. There is a kind of blankness about her, like a canvas. She is much smaller than Charlotte. Her hair is dark. She sits curled up in a towel, feet tucked under her. Her lips form a slight pout; she shows some discontent. Her wrists look so fragile, as if they could break *with a snap. While Charlotte looks at the sunset, the girl looks at Charlotte. She is assessing the flawless skin, the full breasts, the long, long legs. She is thinking about the house filled with treasures—tables inlaid with mother-of-pearl, jade dragons, cloisonné vases, authentic Impressionist landscapes in carved frames. She is thinking about the closet filled with Balenciaga and Dior, the rows of bags and shoes. I know what women think—after all these years I should. She wants everything my Charlotte has. This in itself makes her appealing to me. I want to take her in my arms and comfort her. I can hear her voice now, soft and feathery across the garden.*

"On nights like this, when everything's so beautiful, I want to live forever."

Charlotte says, "Don't say that, Em." Her voice is tense.

The girl reminds me of someone else, too. Not just my young Charlotte. She reminds me of my maker, the one who took me in my madness and discontent and gave me the world and then abandoned me. Abandoned me, but with all the tools I needed to survive every destructive force that could befall the mortal earth.

And then a thought crosses my mind. Maybe I do not really

need Charlotte anymore. Maybe a substitute would suffice. And if I take someone Charlotte loves, in a way she will still be mine.

Although it does not always work, although they do not know it, I might be able to give each of them what they most desire.

The Loneliness of Beautiful Things

I love beautiful old things. They create the illusion that they will last forever, that I will not be alone.

I live in a house filled with them. The house is in the Palisades, overlooking the Pacific Ocean. The Pacific is not unlike my eyes—sometimes sparkling blue and sometimes gray and sometimes dark. It is even older than the things and will last forever, or at least as long as anything else.

The house is a villa with white walls and a coral-tiled roof. It stands behind banks of red roses. There is an entryway with a marble parquet floor, a Ming vase and a painted Chinese cabinet filled with carved opium pipes. On the walls are paintings by Monet and Picasso. Upstairs, in the round master bedroom, is a statue of Quan Yin, the Chinese goddess of compassion, that is almost as tall as I am and painted in faded jade and teal and rose. She lies on a green silk divan because she is broken and cannot sit up on her own. There is a Louis XIV chair of gold and tattered white damask in the powder room and an old Louis Vuitton steamer trunk filled with dress-up clothes. My perfume bottle collection covers the quartz countertops. Most of them are collector's items. Ambergris, labdanum and old rose in crystal teardrops, silver filigreed rosettes. I must always use a lot of perfume to hide the fact that my body has no scent of its own.

I tell everyone that my parents are away, living in Europe. People pity me, but mostly they feel envy. I have all the luxury and freedom a girl my age could want.

They just don't know that I have lived for almost a century.

People want to be me. They think that the way I look and the things I have are enviable. My hair is naturally blond. I read online that the blond gene will soon become extinct. The last blonds will be in Norway or Denmark. Then there will be none left.

I am five feet ten. At the time I was made, this was extremely tall for a girl. My parents worried that I would scare off suitors. Nowadays it is not so extreme.

I am very thin. At the time I was made, this was not considered such a desirable trait. Now it is strived for in a frenzied fashion.

I have broad, bony shoulders. My hips and large breasts have always served me well, except, unfortunately, for the main purpose for which they were designed. No child will ever come from this body, although sometimes I dream of a child, a little girl, to care for.

My large, voluptuous lips are naturally very pink. My eyes are large, heavy-lidded and, as previously mentioned, the colors of the Pacific Ocean. I am often told I have the look of someone who has been awakened from a long, dream-filled sleep.

I move jaggedly and without much grace, but no one seems to mind this at all. They are busy looking at my breasts and long legs, my lips and nostrils and eyes.

I dress mostly in antique-lace blouses or silk gowns, tight blue designer jeans, high-heeled Spanish leather boots and ancient necklaces of giant Chinese amber beads or Egyptian turquoise and gold. I line my eyes with kohl and paint my pink lips red. I wear my naturally blond hair loose and long, or piled up on my head with stray tendrils, or in many little braids.

People want to be me. But I am like that Quan Yin lying prone in my bedroom. No one understands the extent of my loneliness.

Emily Floating

Something terrible has happened to Emily Rosedale.

Emily Rosedale did not have blond hair, blue eyes, big pink lips, big breasts, a lavish wardrobe (at home she liked to wear cutoff jean shorts, her brother's *Star Wars* T-shirts and woolen socks) or a house of her own stuffed with beautiful antiques. This is what she had: sad brown eyes, brown ringlets, ballet lessons, a love of classic novels, delicacy, kindness, innocence—in spite of what had happened to her—a mother who loved her but who did not protect her when she needed it most and a boyfriend named Jared Dorian Pierce.

Emily Rosedale was found in her bathtub with slit wrists. They say it was suicide.

Like Jared Pierce, I, too, loved Emily Rosedale. I can say that I loved her as much as I have loved anyone, except one other, in these long years.

We met in our English class, where I sat bored, daydreaming, examining my perfectly manicured vermilion nails and answering the teacher's queries without having to think, as I have read the material numerous times. Emily was the only one who had anything interesting to say. She always seemed to have an innate understanding of the heroine's fatal flaw.

I noticed that her ringlets would fit perfectly around my fingers. I imagined gently tugging on them, feeling them straighten and then bounce back. She turned one day while I was admiring her curls, turned suddenly and for no apparent reason, and smiled at me over her small shoulder with a sweet, wry curve of her lips.

That was when I sniffed the first whiff of the blood inside her. That is when I saw the true color of her, shining around her head. She was white, white light, but at the very edges a rim of darkness like the blood-red trimming a pale rose.

One day I invited her over to study for a test. Instead of studying we had steak tartar in my kitchen of blue and yellow Venetian tile. The food made her squeamish, but she ate it anyway and drank the red wine I gave her. I drank my special red, the kind I get from my dealer; it resembles a dark Bordeaux. Then we swam naked in my long blue pool with the sea gods spouting jets. The water was warm; it was late spring and you could smell the imaginings of summer and see in the clear distance the ocean that is not unlike my eyes. Emily had undressed shyly, slipping quickly into the pool; her body was smaller and paler than I had thought. She splashed in the water like a child and stayed there until evening came from the east to sit in my rose garden. When Emily finally got out, her lips were blue and her fingers wrinkled with white whorls. I wrapped her in my thickest white bathrobe—stolen, during one of my many visits to New York, from the Plaza Hotel—and brought her inside.

We drank more of our libations, dressed up in gowns from my trunk and danced to Portishead in my sunken living room. She had chosen a white satin ball gown with a tattered skirt, white elbow-length kid gloves with tiny pearl buttons and a diamond tiara. I wore a white velvet cape with a white fox collar over a tulle evening dress covered in beaded blossoms.

She said, "What is it like to have everything?" Her voice was soft, but I heard the slightest edge to it.

I took her hand in mine and twirled her around like a ballerina on a child's jewelry box.

"Tell me!" she insisted.

"What makes you think I have everything?"

"Oh, come on, you just want to hear me say it! You're a genius, you look like a supermodel and you live in a palace!"

She danced away from me, around the Tang horses on the inlaid table. In some ways she reminded me of myself so long ago. The freedom, the sweetness and the underlying restlessness and discontent. It was as if we had known each other forever.

"I don't have everything. Believe me. You may have everything yourself and just not know it yet."

Emily shook her head and stopped dancing. "I don't," she said. She sat down on the couch and I joined her. Her eyes were bright with agitation.

"What's wrong?" I asked her. I wanted to stroke her hair to calm her. I noticed that the light-blue polish on her toenails was chipped. I wanted to repaint them for her.

"Charlotte. I was going to tell you something. I don't know you that well. It's probably too much." It was a statement, but I heard the question mark at the end. She hoped I would insist.

"You can tell me," I said. "I understand about secrets." How I wanted then to let Emily know who I really was. I felt so close to her. So close. Maybe just because I hadn't had a girl sit beside me in such a long time, but still. I could smell the soap she had used in my bathroom, and the more elusive scent of her skin beneath it.

I poured us more wine, and she took a large gulp, grimaced as it went down.

"I couldn't tell my mom, even."

"I understand," I said, remembering my mother's wan face before I left her. She never knew my secret, either.

Then Emily told me that her mother's last boy-friend had raped her the night before he left her mom two years before.

The only one Emily had ever told was Jared Pierce. She was afraid to admit that being with Jared did make her feel as if she had everything, in spite of what had been taken from her.

"Meeting him felt like it saved my life," she told me. "Before that I didn't think anything mattered. I used to go to sleep wishing I wouldn't wake up in the morning."

"I understand," I said.

"Now I want to live forever. If I had one wish it would be to live forever with the one I love."

She said she had never known you could love anyone that much, for eternity or enough to die for, like the characters in her favorite novels. She had thought it was just a fiction.

I told her, "No, that is real."

Believe me. I know. But even if I wanted to die for someone, it wouldn't be that easy.

They just keep dying for me.

Emily, none of this is worth it. Not this endangered blond hair, not this house full of shining things, the velvets and pearls and shiny red-soled shoes of fortune, not even this beautiful curse of immortality. What you had, even with the pain—that was life. What I have, especially now, without you, without the other one I loved and lost, is just living. Dead.

Jared Dorian Pierce

*H*is tall, even hunched over like that. Long arms and legs, the bony wrists dangling from his shirtsleeves. Black hair—straight, combed back or falling in his face. Even unshaven, his chin is still defined. His eyes are dark green and slanted, feline, under his dark glasses. Emily had told me he was adopted, his heritage a mix that embarrassed him, although it was what made him so beautiful. Dressed carefully in white cotton T-shirts and torn Levi's, sometimes a leather jacket, black biker boots. Not like all the surfer boys around here in their shorts and flip-flops, but he can surf, too. He walked with her everywhere, protective; sat sullenly outside her ballet studio every afternoon to give her a ride home on his motorcycle. All the girls wanted a boy like that. Someone so beautiful to wait for them.

I tried to hide it from both of them, but I, too, wanted a Jared Pierce for myself, the way I had wanted William when we first met.

Jared Pierce was an artist. A real one. What I had always wanted to be, and perhaps, once, could have been. He painted Emily's portrait and wrote songs for her on his guitar. Sang them to her in her darkened room before he kissed her. She heard about herself in the songs, saw her face and body in the portraits and hardly recognized that angel, but it reminded her of how she appeared to him. He had even painted her as a little girl from an old photo. That was her favorite of the portraits. In it she looked very small except for her long white neck and looming, womanly eyes.

✿ ✿ ✿

I came to find him the day after the funeral. I knew where he would be, on the beach in front of his house. The police had already questioned him and let him go. You'd have thought his family and friends would have him on suicide watch after what had happened, but he was alone. Not that he had any friends. Except for Emily, who was gone.

And me?

I wondered.

The day was bright, but I felt a menacing gray gloom, turning raggedy black at the edges, veined with black. I stripped off my shoes and walked barefoot across the damp sand at the shore, feeling it squish between my toes. He sat hunched on the beach, wearing jeans, a thermal and a sweatshirt with the sleeves pulled down over his hands, protection against the cool wind. The light was flashing whiteness, and I never feel safe like that. Maybe it's just psychological, based on all the mythology. The idea that we can't be out in the day wasn't even in the original lore (it came from the movies), but I still dress carefully in the sun—a big white hat and long-sleeved zip-up shirt in a thick white sunproof fabric. Layers of sunscreen. You just never know.

I came up behind Jared and saw he was holding something white in his hands, holding it up to his face.

I said his name.

He jumped and turned to see me, crumpling the white thing in his large hand. "Fuck!"

"I'm sorry if I startled you."

"Charlotte." He looked at me in a way I had seen him look at me before, when Emily was alive, but I had denied it then. It was as if he could see beyond my surface to what lay beneath. As if he could see the layers of darkness and, way beneath that, the last flicker of light that might still be there.

"Can I sit here?" I asked, and he nodded, so I sat beside him on the sand. He was unshaven and looked as if he hadn't bathed in days.

"I'm so sorry," I said. Together we looked out to

the horizon. I couldn't meet his gaze. The intensity was too much.

He hung his head between his knees.

"I know how you must feel," I told him.

Then he looked up at me and I couldn't look away. His eyes were flashing like the light on the water. For a moment I could not breathe. "You don't know," he said.

In his upset, Jared had loosened his grip on the piece of fabric in his hands. I saw that it was a white cotton bra. He shoved it into his sweatshirt pocket and his face reddened.

"I loved her, too," I said.

"You don't understand any of this," he replied, and suddenly he was not seeing into me anymore. He was not seeing me at all.

Jared Pierce was wrong about me not understanding. Before I was this thing I am now, I was a girl, like Emily Rosedale. I was a person, like Jared Pierce, and I had also lost the one person I loved most.

The Twin

Charles and I cantered over the meadow like wild horses, whinnying uncannily; we both had that talent. I had violets in my hair. The wind blew the clouds across the high blue.

Charles was my twin, long-limbed and blue-eyed like me. But his hair was black, like my mother's. Black Irish. And I had my father's hair. He was from pale Puritan stock. They burned witches at the stake in Salem. Think of the irony! How I would later wonder—as a descendant of those who would have ripped my kind to shreds—what would become of me?

The day shone; if the wind had a color, that day it would have been light green. That was before I could see the true colors of things, before I could smell so keenly. But even then there was the scent of meadowlands and streams, violets and grape hyacinths; my brother.

Charles and Charlotte. The beautiful ones who had everything. Who had each other. I had something else then. I had the ability to feel what Charles was feeling; to know what he was thinking, what he did when he was away from me; to see what might happen even when he was out of my sight. When he cut himself, my skin throbbed. When he missed me, my heart fluttered. If I stood close enough to him and closed my eyes, I could see images of things that he had done when he was away from me. If I concentrated hard enough, I could even send him psychic messages. *Meet me in the garden. Meet me in the woods, under the biggest white oak by the brook.* And Charles had the same empathic and psychic abilities as I did. Our thoughts were powerful in an almost supernatural way, but we never thought anything of it; it was as natural to us as the color of our eyes. And this power never worked on anyone except the other.

We lived in a large stone house with a tower from which my father surveyed the planets. My mother created what she called her "pageants," decorations for every season. In winter there was a fir tree covered with candles, and holly wreaths on every door. Handmade stockings hanging from the mantel, silver paper snowflakes dangling from the beams, feasts of goose and plum pudding. In spring there were baskets dripping with flowers, and young animals birthed in the garden, in the henhouse—kittens in my mother's linen drawer. She made me a May Queen gown and I danced around the maypole with ribbons in my hair. Charles teased me; he would only dance alone with me in the meadows when no one was looking.

One summer day, when we were thirteen, the humidity was so high it soaked our hair, our clothes.

"Let's swim!" Charles announced.

"I don't have my bathing costume."

"It's too hot for that!"

He took my hand and we ran through the tall, buzzing grass to the glade, then down to the river. It tumbled the stones at its depths, polishing them. Charles removed his linen suit and tossed it on the bank, then flung himself into the water.

"Come join me, Charlotte! It's wonderful."

I stood shyly under the trees, dappled with green and golden sunlight. My heart was pounding, and I couldn't tell if I was feeling his excitement or my own. We used to bathe together as children, but it had been years. My dress had so many tiny buttons it felt as if I stood there forever while he splashed like a fish, coming up to grin at me. Finally I hung my dress on a branch and waded in. I felt his gaze across the water. I took off my camisole, my knickers. I walked into that water as naked as when we were born.

When we got out of the river that day, we put on

each other's clothes. We were the same size. He was so beautiful in my white linen dress. And his linen suit felt so natural hanging off my shoulders and hips. Almost as if I were wearing him.

We never told anyone of this indiscretion. It was our secret. It was one more perfect moment I would lose when he was gone.

Charles Charles Charles Emerson. Where did you go? Why couldn't you have received this curse along with me? We would live forever all over the world, buying and selling our beautiful things, changing our homes, our lovers, our coiffures with the ages. But always together.

Charles contracted rheumatic fever and died when we were fifteen. I was not yet cursed; there was nothing I could do to help him. The night the disease entered his body, burning him up from within, I woke in a sweat, screaming. Our mother came to me first.

"Go to Charles!" I shouted. But it was too late.

There was nothing that could have been done anyway.

You have visions, you have powerful thoughts, I told myself. I sat by my Charles's bedside and tried to imagine him healthy again, running beside me through the meadows. But my visions and thoughts were useless; they did not save him. And they died with Charles. I wish that I had died then, too, so as to have ended the neverending story of Charlotte Emerson.

My father withdrew to the study in his tower to watch the planets. My mother lay catatonic on Charles's bed. No one could get her to move. We had to bring her her meals on a tray and spoon-feed her so she would not starve to death.

How did I, Charlotte, twin sister of the deceased, cope with such a loss? I stood at his grave in a black dress with a high collar, a black lace veil over my dripping face. The old stone graveyard where all our ancestors were buried, where one day everyone thought that I, too, would finally be put to rest. I imagined my headstone beside Charles's; I did not at that time conceive of a husband, alive or dead. The slabs of gray marble, the twining rose briars, the day too bright and blue for the death of a boy. I ran out into the fields, tearing my lace dress on brambles, my hair wild around my face, my cheeks streaked with mud and tears. I ran and ran, hoping my heart would explode, but it had become too strong from trying to keep up with Charles all those years. It betrayed me and has continued to do so for almost a century.

What else did I do? What would you do? If William Stone Eliot had materialized one Halloween evening, dressed as the devil, more handsome than any young man you had ever seen except the one who was gone, and offered you everything, would you not have accepted?

I told none of this to Jared Pierce, of course. I knew he was ill with sorrow. I accepted his scorn.

When I looked at him, I saw a strange vision, like

the ones I used to have when I was mortal. I saw Jared Pierce stripping off his clothing and walking into the sea.

I said, "If you ever need me, come to me. Maybe I can help in some way."

He looked as if he might spit. "Just leave me alone," he said

There was nothing more I could do. Before he could say anything more, I was gone down the beach, under the hazardous sun.

The Devil in Disguise

*M*y parents were concerned that I might never recover from the death of my brother, and they were so grief-stricken themselves that they gave me much more freedom than I might otherwise have enjoyed. Without their knowledge, I visited a spiritualist, who introduced me to psychography, the art of automatic writing. She said I could communicate with Charles this way, and whether the words I wrote were from him or my own unconscious, they comforted me. They recounted our childhood together, and sometimes they were ominous, full of warnings about the future. I didn't care—anything to connect me to him was welcomed.

I spent my days in the meadows with an easel and canvas, painting the wildflowers and the sky that Charles loved. Sometimes I painted the figures of a boy and a girl running through the landscape, but I never showed these images to anyone. Sometimes I practiced my own form of witchcraft in the woods, using twigs and flowers to make an effigy of a boy and holding him in my arms, breathing into his petal mouth, trying to bring him back to life. I returned home late at night with mud on my shoes and leaves in my hair, and no one asked where I had been.

And when our friends hosted a costume ball on All Hallows' Eve, a year after my brother's death, my sorrowful mother, no longer so protective of me, allowed me to attend.

Gwendolyn and Gerald Doolittle had a gentleman

visiting them at the time. He was only five years older than me, but he had already been on tour in Europe and had published a number of poems in a literary review, to much acclaim. Everyone whispered about his shady reputation, but he was also notoriously handsome, and there was a great deal of fussing and primping among the young ladies that night; they all had secret hopes of gaining his favor.

It was impossible not to recognize him at once in his red satin cloak, with his dark curls styled into two small horns on either side of his head. He even wore custom-made leather boots with cleft heels. I felt ridiculously underdressed in a black taffeta gown my mother had made for me, even with the crow-feather mask over my eyes. I had worn only black for the entire year following Charles's death. That night I wished for the first time for a dress of silver, like the stars my father worshipped and, since Charles's death, seemed to love more than his wife and daughter—a dress to ignite William Stone Eliot's fancy.

The Doolittles' ballroom was bordered by a glass atrium that opened out onto a sunken garden filled with fountains and mossy grottoes. I stepped outside to cool off; there were beads of sweat on my forehead. It wasn't ladylike to perspire, but I had danced in a frenzied fashion all night anyway, with any partner who would have me, hoping to relieve the pain in my heart.

William Stone Eliot had danced with every girl, it seemed, except for me. Maybe it was the black dress, or perhaps the death that followed me around like my brother's shade. I knew I was as pretty as any girl there, though, and for the first time in my life I was grateful for my physical attributes as a means to an end, rather than just for the joy and freedom they had provided me when I ran on my long legs through the fields with Charles or felt the wind like fingers in my hair.

Though I had learned the power of my thoughts as a child, communicating telepathically with Charles, my faith had been fully shaken when he died. If I had any power at all, how could I not have prevented the loss of my twin? Why didn't my love and my spells and effigies bring his spirit back to me, even in the body of another? Now I decided to test my powers again on the strange man who had not yet noticed me. Maybe I could be distracted from my loss if I could call the sought-after William Stone Eliot to my side.

Sure enough, I heard someone behind me, felt a hand on my shoulder, and turned around. He was very tall, with a body like a marble statue and a chiseled face trimmed with a neat beard. His black eyes gleamed, and he flashed a smile of small but sharp white teeth.

I felt a weakness in my knees and took a step back.

Now I wonder, did I call him to me or was it the other way around? Had he sent me out alone into the garden to receive him?

"Charlotte Emerson," he said softly, holding out his hand. "It's a pleasure to make your acquintance."

"And yours," I said.

"May I call you something else? 'Charlotte' feels too formal, too heavy for you."

"I don't have another name."

"Then I'll give you one. They call me Stone. And you shall be Char." I stood transfixed by his eyes as he gently removed my glove and pressed his lips to my naked hand. His mouth felt full and soft, and I shivered with sensation.

He took my arm, and we walked down the garden path.

"Do you know the origin of All Hallows' Eve?" he asked me, and then continued before I could answer. "The ancients believed that the night was taking over as the days grew shorter. They feared that demons and evil spirits were coming out of hiding, stealing the light. So they disguised themselves as their enemies in order to be safe." He scrutinized my dress. "Do you feel safe, Mademoiselle, in your mask and black gown?"

"Perfectly. But I see you must rely on the dress of

a devil to protect you," I answered, as we continued our stroll.

"Ah, wit as well as beauty. Quite a combination."

"But alas, no demon boots upon her feet."

"That can be easily remedied. I see you wear the slippers of a pampered girl. What do you do with your days, Char Emerson?"

I stopped walking and resisted the impulse to stamp my foot.

"I study," I said coolly, putting my black glove back on, "with my father. I do needlepoint. I dance. I walk in the gardens." My voice went up a note in spite of my best efforts.

"Ah. A lady of leisure. I was correct."

"I paint," I said, bristling even more. "I write. I will be a respected artist one day."

His tone softened. "Yes, good, that's good. And I assume you'd like to learn more about the arts."

"I have a tutor."

"But what about the colleges? There's so much to

learn, my dear, especially if you want to be a respected artist, as you say. And what about traveling? I assume you've been abroad."

"Just once. I took a European tour with my parents. And Charles."

"Charles?"

"My brother."

I took off my mask and gazed out across the banks of dark rosebushes, imagining a boy in a white suit running through the moonlight.

Stone was watching my face. "Are you all right, Mademoiselle?"

"My brother died not long ago," I said, curling my hands around the ornate iron railing.

He moved closer to me.

"I'm sorry."

I hung my head for a moment, then brushed away the tear that clung to my cheek and looked up at him.

"I am going to Italy this summer before I return to

my studies," he said. "Perhaps you could join me."

This startled me and broke the spell for a moment.

"My parents would never agree!" I answered. "But you are bold to think of it."

"I am very bold," said William Eliot. "And you would be surprised what I can get people to agree to, Mademoiselle."

He was right. He got my parents to agree, as long as I would be chaperoned by the Doolittles. At the time, I believed it was their grief that made them blind. Perhaps. But William Eliot had powers I could not have imagined as I stood in that dark garden waiting for my life to begin, having no idea that it was only never-ending.

Nightmare

*M*y closet is really more like a room filled with designer clothes. Tweedy Chanel suits, Yves Saint Laurent satin smoking jackets, Dior chiffon gowns, Balenciaga taffetas. I like to say the name of those masters; they have a magical, incantory sound. Emily liked to go into that room and run her hands over everything, feeling the textures of lace, velvet and silk. My shoes were too big for her, but she took them out of their boxes and their linen pouches and tried them on anyway, like a little girl playing dress-up, teetering around in the chunky platforms, the spike-heeled pointed pumps, the strappy sandals. We even looked through my lingerie—the boxes of antique French-lace bras and satin panties embroidered with tiny rosettes and tied at the hips with ribbons. Sometimes I would see a tense look on Emily's face as she explored. Perhaps it was envy, but I hoped that it was not. One reason I never got close to anyone was because of this familiar look. There were girls I had met over the years whom I wanted to know better. But they always seemed to resent me for my material wealth and perhaps for my appearance, my apparent power over boys. I could never explain that what I had meant nothing compared to being truly alive. Even though Emily did not know my story, I sensed that she was different, that she somehow understood what was really important. Maybe the look on her face only meant that she was sad because she did not have what I did, not that she wanted to take it from me. Maybe I just wished this to be so.

Once, when she was trying on my shoes, I asked her what was wrong.

"It's just insane how much stuff you have. You're so lucky."

"You're welcome to borrow any of it," I said, and the look on her face softened.

"No one has ever been so generous. Ever."

"You deserve it, You deserve to have everything you want."

"I do," she said. "I have Jared and I have you."

One night I dressed her in a Courrèges silver 1960s mini shift dress and go-go boots, and we went to a club in Santa Monica. My outfit matched hers, but it was in gold. I had tailored the silver dress to fit her, and she let me put makeup on her face and douse her with French perfume. She looked beautiful, like my little doll, and she smelled like Paris, especially to my sensitive nostrils, but she kept checking her reflection in her compact mirror and wrinkling her nose at herself.

"I'm so much shorter than you are," she said.

"You're perfect."

The bouncer let our fake IDs pass with a wink. He thought he was doing me a big favor, but he had no idea that I was three times as old as he was.

"I guess he thought we were cute," I said.

Emily rolled her eyes. "He thought you were Gisele Bündchen. Of course we got in."

"Okay, Miss Natalie Portman. Or are you Keira Knightley?"

"Shut up, Gisele."

The club was small and boxy, but the music was good. Goldfrapp and Ladytron pounding away in a neopsychedelic trance. Emily seemed a little withdrawn, so I bought her a drink, and when she'd loosened up I pulled her out on the floor. I could feel people watching us, trying to figure out our story. I liked that feeling; it used to thrill me to walk in somewhere with William and capture everyone's attention.

I told Emily, and she said, "They're watching you.

I might as well be invisible."

I took her hands in mine and leaned closer, speaking into her ear while the music vibrated up through our feet.

"You have no idea how pretty and perfect you are. I don't want to hear anything more about that."

Emily hugged me. "It's not true, but thank you for saying it."

I kissed her cheek. There was sweat on her face. She had her period; I could tell. I could smell her blood.

We'd fallen asleep on my bed in our clothes, watching a movie called *The Dead Girl* by candlelight. It was about how the discovery of a prostitute's body made several other female characters realize that they were the living dead.

She told me later that I had cried out in my sleep, "Don't leave me, Emily!"

"Wake up, Char. You're dreaming."

Her hands were like sun-warmed petals against my

cheeks. As she leaned over me, her breath was even warmer. Sweet. I opened my eyes. Her pupils looked huge, and her lashes made shadows on her cheeks. Her curls fell loosely about her face. The candles had burned down to a low flicker.

I gripped her tiny wrists. "Don't leave!"

"What were you dreaming about?"

"I didn't want you to die," I said. My heart was still pounding, and the back of my neck felt clammy and cold.

"I'm fine," Emily whispered, putting her arms around me. "I'm right here."

"But someday you will die." I knew I sounded like a child, but I couldn't help myself. It was as if I were still dreaming.

Emily laughed softly. She rested her curly, soft head on my shoulder. "Someday. We all will. Even you, Miss Perfect."

"Shhh. Don't call me that." The panic rose in me again. I couldn't explain to her that this idea of perfection was no joke. It was a deadly thing.

"Oh, sorry," she said breezily. "Miss Perfect with all the perfect clothes."

"Stop." My jaw and fists clenched. I wanted to silence her. It was the first time she had ever really angered me. The heat of it flashed at my temples and in my throat. She had no idea who I was, and if she really knew, I was afraid she would leave me. I would be alone again.

"Char? I've never seen you like this. What happened?"

"It was so real. You were dead. And," I added, saying too much, "I wasn't ever going to be."

"That doesn't sound so bad in my opinion," she laughed. "I'd like to be immortal. In this house. With you. We could dance and dance and never stop."

I smelled the rich red wine of her blood again then. Like tiny grapes. Plums. Berries. A bit of cocoa. A hint of cinnamon. A tang of iron.

"Don't say that!"

"Maybe Jared could come, too."

I put my hand over her mouth. Her lips felt like a small wet fruit. But with sharp seed teeth. For a second something showed in her eyes. It was fear, but I hadn't recognized it immediately in Emily's trusting face, and I moved my hand away.

"Sorry," I said. "Just don't say that around me. Don't joke about it."

"All right, Char. I won't. You just need to calm down, okay? Let's make you some chamomile tea or something."

The candles had all burned down to their wicks. My mouth felt like sand. She got up and padded on her sock feet into the kitchen. I followed her like a pet, inhaling her scent. I had very little strength left. Very little willpower. It gets exhausting being a girl. Having to monitor everything you say and do, everything you consume—even, if someone is sleeping beside you, your very dreams.

Pretty Dead

Some very strange things have been happening to me since Emily died.

For one thing, there was the broken nail. My nails do not break. Ever. But here it was, split at the quick, the day after Emily's death, ruining the perfection of my hand. It terrified me, because I did not understand, but it also gave me a strange sense of relief. I wondered if it was perhaps possible that somehow the curse could reverse itself, that somehow I could become mortal. I remembered reading something in one of William's old books. It was a story of a vampire named Mariette and her handmaid, Camille. Mariette wanted to escape her curse. When she gave in to her urges and attacked Camille, Mariette's maker intervened at the last moment and changed Camille into his eternal partner. Mariette became a human once again, graced with mortality and death.

Could vampires become human? Could this, weird as it sounded but no less strange than my life so far, be happening to me?

The next morning, I went to wash my face and there in the mirror (yes, we have reflections) was my face with a difference. A small red bump on my forehead. I believe they call it a zit. I wouldn't know. Again I felt terror and a queasy relief. I patted makeup over the offending pimple and went to school.

And finally, there was the blood. There was the cow blood I used to drink that I no longer wanted. I had switched to wine. And there was the blood staining my white undergraments on the third morning after Emily's death. The bleeding didn't stop. At first

I thought, *Oh, I am dying! Charles, Charles, I am dying at last. Too cowardly for a stake through the heart, but now I will come to you anyway.*

Something was happening to me. Vampires do not break their nails. Their skin does not break out; they do not bleed. But all these things had happened to me when I was a real girl.

Before I was just pretty dead.

Watch

I was worried about Jared Pierce. When I walked away from him on the beach that day, I wondered if I would ever see him again. He was in class the following afternoon, but I was still concerned.

What is worry? A mild anguish in the chest. A gnawing sensation. Repeated thoughts whirling in the brain. I had worried about Charles constantly when we were little. I did have some kind of intuition about what would happen to him, but at the beginning I believed everyone turned fearful thoughts of loved ones over in their brains, polishing them in this way, making them smoother and more precise, until the incident occurred or was prevented. Would he fall and hurt himself? Would a bee sting him? What if he got lost on his way home? When I had these thoughts, I found out later that my fears had come to pass. Or had almost come to pass: the bee, for instance, hadn't actually stung him, though it had circled close and frightened him the day I thought of it. But for some reason I never thought that Charles might catch a fever and die. Perhaps that fear was too much for my mortal soul to comprehend.

When the bell rang, I followed Jared discreetly down the hall. I followed him home to the trailer park that day. Emily had told me that after Jared's father left, his mother didn't want to take her children out of the school district, and the trailer was all she could afford. I waited, parked on the street, while he went inside and then came out again. I got out of my Porsche and followed him to the beach. I hid behind a sandbank and watched him for a long time. He did nothing but sit on the sand and stare into the distance. After a while my eyes closed. Moments later I opened them to clear an image from my mind. It was of Jared standing, taking off his clothes, and walking naked into the ocean. But no, there he was, dressed and still sitting on the sand. I remembered the visions I'd had of Charles—it had been so long since I had seen images of what was to come. I wondered how it was possible for them to return. Was it that I had just never felt so connected to anyone else? Or was it something in me that had changed when I became what I am now? Was I somehow changing back?

Jared and I sat like that until nightfall, and then I followed him to his trailer and left him reluctantly. I did not trust that he was going to be all right after Emily's death, after what I had seen.

Later that night, unable to sleep, I returned to the trailer. I prowled around its perimeter, peering into the windows. The space was cluttered and dimly lit. A heavyset blond woman reclined on the couch, asleep in front of the glaring television. In one room Jared's younger sister slept in the arms of her boyfriend. The other siblings had moved out. Jared's room was the smallest. I could see him sitting on his bed, holding a piece of white fabric; I recognized Emily's bra, the one he'd had at the beach. Jared took out a bottle of what looked like perfume and sprayed it on the garment. Then he undressed and lay on his bed. I stood mesmerized. The look on his face was not of pleasure but of great sorrow. It sent a tremor through my body.

The crate I was standing on slipped then, and I fell. The clattering sound made Jared jump. He got out of bed, naked, and ran to the window. I vanished into the night, satisfied at least that he was still alive, still able to feel sensations in his body. I thought of his body until dawn. Its golden shade. Its lean musculature. His trunk. His sapling arms. His stark, vulnerable pelvis.

Dark Trick

The next day, just a few days after Emily's death, we learned that my English teacher's husband had died. He'd been diagnosed with a brain tumor, and she'd been missing more and more school, her face sagging farther with grief every day. I had been able to smell his death on her, and I was only waiting for the substitute to arrive. But, even with my sharpened senses, I could not detect who it was going to be. Perhaps my senses were failing me, as they had continually since Emily had been gone.

He walked in wearing a black cotton button-down

shirt, black jeans and heavy black shoes. He had a goatee, and his hair was cropped close. There were tiny marks on his earlobes where they had been pierced. On his wrist was a heavy silver watch.

1920. 2007. It didn't matter. The face was the same.

"I'm Mr. Eliot," he said. "As in T. S. I assume you know who that is?"

He smirked at us. His dark eyes absorbed all the light from the window behind me.

"I know you've all had to deal with Mrs. Harter's situation. It isn't easy to have to watch that every day. Sometimes it's as if you can smell the death on someone."

A few people snickered.

Mr. Eliot stepped closer. He seemed to grow in size as we watched.

"Not funny. I'd think you could appreciate that kind of loss, after what just happened to your classmate."

There was an uncomfortable silence. Mr. Eliot began to roam around the room like an uncaged panther. The students stiffened in their chairs as he passed them.

"But that doesn't mean I'm going to cut you any slack," he snarled. "I'm going to expect a lot out of you. English literature is not about your friends blogging so-called poems on MySpace or even Death Cab for Cutie quotes under their names. Now. T. S. Eliot?" He glanced affectedly at the attendance sheet and then at me. "Charlotte?"

The classroom seemed to darken, as if a cloud had blocked the sun.

I could feel the old, familiar tightening in my throat. The numb tingling in my fingers and toes. The shortness of breath. He'd told me that was how he'd felt when he'd made me. He'd wanted so badly to keep going, to drain me entirely, but he held himself back, offered me his own bleeding wrist. He said this as if it were a sacrifice he'd made for me, as if I were not the sacrifice.

But I am strong, I told myself. *I am wiser now. I have the ability to make others just as he made me.* Then I ran the tip of my thumb along the quick-torn nail. It had only grown back a little. Everything had been changing inside and around me since Emily's death. What was happening? Why had William Eliot returned now, after all this time? I made myself speak, but my voice sounded strangled.

"September 26, 1888, to January 4, 1965. Expatriate. Author of "The Love Song of J. Alfred Prufrock," *The Waste Land, The Hollow Men, Ash Wednesday* and others. Won the Nobel Prize in 1948."

I did my best to appear bored. I even rolled my eyes. He smiled at me.

"I see someone has been listening. You seem wise beyond your years, Miss Emerson. Are you really just seventeen?"

I had the strangest sensation of blood rising to my cheeks, as it had when I was still a girl. But I could no longer blush. At least I hadn't been able to for years.

I got up and walked out of the room. That was when I realized that my armpits were damp; sweat had soaked through my white blouse.

We do not perspire.

As I ran down the corridor, my Prada bootheels clicking, all I could think of was reclining in that Venetian gondola as the sun set, turning the water red. I was eating slices of watermelon, the spongy flesh disintegrating in my mouth. My dress spread out around me in the boat. The buildings were peeling like sunburned flesh. My heart beat a dull dirge in my chest.

"The fallen angels choose only the most beautiful humans to be their fledglings, their disciples," he told me. His cold hands with the silver rings stroked my hair nervously. "Do you know why, my Char?"

"No," I murmured. "Tell me."

"You are a great beauty. Do you know it?"

I gazed up at his face. It was so perfectly chiseled,

as if carved from stone. So white, waxy, masklike in this light. I didn't know what he was yet, but I was beginning to understand. They say that vampires aren't real, that they are a myth that came about during the time of cholera, when the dehydrated bodies looked as if they'd been drained by a beast, but I had always believed in monsters. William was beautiful, too, but he was also something more than that, something ghoulish, although I didn't realize the extent of it. We continued to glide through the red water. He glared at the setting sun. Night was coming, and then he would relax. He was always less agitated in the dark.

"My beauty doesn't matter," I said. "Charles was taken from me because he was too beautiful. Not of this world. Maybe the fallen angels stole him. Because any god worth believing in never would."

"You are too beautiful for this world," he said. "You are perfect, even in your sorrow. Even without your brother."

"I am nothing without him."

"Listen, listen. I didn't tell you the answer to my question. Maybe you are right about Charles. The fallen angels chose only the most beautiful humans to be their disciples because it was an even greater insult to God."

"Fallen angels," I said. "Is that what you are?"

He smiled, but he did not answer.

We were in Rome when we finally succumbed. I say "we" because it seems to me that it was something we did together in Rome in the dark. Something both of us wanted at that time. I had figured out what William was and I wanted to join him. How can you not succumb to such a desire in Rome, in the dark with a fountain spurting outside your window, the shadows long from the white moon?

I was like that moon to William's demon sun. "The moon does not really emit light at all," my father had told me. "It is the sun that is so bright."

I thought of these words as I entered William Stone Eliot's chamber. It had been easy to get away. Gwendolyn Doolittle, my chaperone, was fast asleep. She and her husband had fallen under William's spell. There was no furniture in William's room; only the long black box. There was no one to protect me. From William Eliot. And, perhaps more relevantly, from myself. Maybe the dark trick of being changed into a vampire is not something that is wholly done to you. Is it something that comes when called by the subconscious? Thoughts are powerful. They can bring love. They can bring death. They can bring death in the guise of love, a dark-haired man in heavy trousers and a linen nightshirt less white than his skin, who bows his head to your breast, and bares, and punctures, and ruptures and drains until you are empty and he is full. Then death/love offers you his wrist and you drink until the reverse is true.

The
Philosophical Egg

Why had William returned? Why now, so soon after Emily's death? How had he found me? But more important, why? Was he going to try to take me away with him? I remembered when he and I last lived in Los Angeles together. It was 1994, the year of the Northridge earthquake. We were in a ranch house in Laurel Canyon at the time. It sprawled, multileveled, down the side of a smoggy, wild-flowered hillside. At about four thirty in the morning we woke in a storm of glass.

William mumbled, "Oh, fuck," and went back to sleep. I stumbled around in my bare feet, picking up shards of windows and picture frames. Later William watched the destruction on TV, and he wanted to drive around and look at it, too. I remember the story of one old woman who was crushed to death by a chest of drawers. I kept thinking of her. There's usually one who stands out in each disaster. One whose face I remember.

After the earthquake we didn't bother to fix the windows. We sold the house as it was and moved to a Craftsman in Venice, where we painted the walls of the main room red and wrote poetry all over them with a Sharpie pen. We were there for only a few months before we left for Seattle. But I knew the house with the red room was where William would go if he returned to L.A.

Every once in a while, over the years, I'd drive past the house and see if anyone was living there. It had remained abandoned, boarded up, and I was relieved.

He can't find me, I thought. *He won't guess I'm here. My blood has no scent to give me away.*

I was wrong.

I had no scent, but I was still living in the world, and when William was determined about something, no one could stop him. Besides, six years is nothing to spend searching when you are as old as he is.

With William's return I no longer felt safe leaving my house. I stayed locked in, as if it were a coffin.

No, I do not sleep in a coffin. I sleep in a big bed with a headboard of an antique silk Japanese wedding kimono, embroidered with flowers and cranes, though sometimes, I admit, I imagine climbing into my Louis Vuitton steamer trunk. But I have trained myself to behave as normally as possible.

Still, I do think about coffins. Not the rotting, rat-infested boxes of Nosferatu. Long cherrywood caskets lined with pink satin. Golden hinges and locks, a golden key. How I would look laid out that way with my hair spread about my shoulders, over my breasts, in the sheer white Victorian lace.

How did Emily look in her coffin under the earth? I tried not to imagine it. I was so alone without her, my only companion. I kept thinking I heard her laughing in my house. I dreamed of chasing her down the corridors at school, touching her warm, bony shoulder. The girl with the brown curls turned around, but just as in the films it was never her. She was gone, and I had no one left to turn to unless Jared Pierce became my friend.

No, I do not sleep in a coffin. The night he made me, William Stone Eliot showed me the huge, black, shiny one he slept in. He told me that alchemists used to call coffins "the philosophical egg." "A place of transmutation," he said. "Entrapment and rebirth. In what way, my darling, will you be transformed?"

I wondered why I was transforming now, after the death of my best and only friend. Was there some kind of connection? I thought of the broken nail, the pimple that had started to heal, the five days of blood. All this change and no coffin to speak of, though perhaps one awaited me at last.

The Fires

It was October, but the air was hot. The Santa Anas were sweeping wildfire through the hills of Malibu. Thousands of people had evacuated. Every morning the city advised us to hose down our roofs. Movie stars and diet gurus had already lost their mansions. The air was black with smoke, and strangely even I could feel it in my newly vulnerable throat.

A few days after William's return, Jared Pierce came to my door. He stood there on the porch with his hands in his pockets. His back was slumped. His pupils looked large and glazed.

"I need to talk to you," he said.

And I let him in.

We sat on the velvet couch where I used to sit with Emily. She always tucked her feet up under her. She reminded me of a little bird perched on a nest. Quick, bright eyes, quick shoulders like wings.

I offered Jared some wine, but he refused. He sat tensely upright, looking suspiciously around the room.

"Why were you following me?"

"What?" I widened my eyes innocently.

"Don't act like you don't know. I saw you following me. I want to know why." He moved closer to me. His gaze was menacing, but I saw that really he was just afraid.

"I was worried," I said. "I didn't want you to hurt yourself."

He stared at me for a long time. I felt heat rising to my cheeks again. How strange.

"How did you know?"

"Know what?"

"What I was going to do?"

"So you were going to . . ."

"I changed my mind."

"Jared . . ." I wanted to reach out and touch his arm, but I kept my hands still.

He took my hand as if it were a piece of sculpture or a scientific experiment, turned it, examined the skin, ran a finger along one visible vein.

"I know what you are," he finally said.

I pulled my hand away and stood up.

The warmth continued to move through my body. I couldn't have explained it then, but instead of anxiety I felt a sense of relief. No one had ever understood before. Somehow it seemed that Jared had figured it out. I felt less alone in that moment. Even Emily hadn't known what I was. Only Jared. But how could he know? In any case, I couldn't let him see how his accusation was affecting me.

"Oh, really? And who is that? I mean, *what* is that?

71

I'm noticing you called me a what," I bantered, trying to gather myself.

He looked away, and for a moment I felt I had gained the upper hand in spite of what he had charged me with.

"Don't make me say it," he mumbled.

"Why? Are you afraid to sound ridiculous?" I poured myself more wine and sat in a chair across from him.

"All I know is that I don't want to be here this way. Without her. It sucked enough before. This whole fucking planet. Without her I can't do it. I need your help. No one else can help me."

"How?" I asked softly.

"I know what you are," he said again.

I took a long sip of wine. It was real wine, not the cow blood I usually drank.

"Just say it, then."

"Fuck! Okay. You want me to say it? The walking dead? Child of the night? Night angel? Bloodsucker?

Daughter of Dracula? You choose."

"I actually prefer the V word," I said. "It sounds awful, but it has a lot of power. Come to think of it, that applies to both V words."

Jared's body jolted forward as if someone had jerked his invisible marionette strings. "Make me one!"

I knew better than to make a joke about the second V word at that moment. But I honestly wished he was asking me for that instead. Human girls don't have it easy in a culture that makes their beautiful burgeoning sexuality sound ugly and taboo, but at least they don't have to go through this. I finished my wine to the dregs. A queer dizziness came over me.

"Let's just say I am one. Why would you want me to change you? You'd have to live without Emily forever." I looked out the windows. Fires were raging in the distance. Just a few weeks before, I would have felt the heat and heard the crackle as if I had been standing in the center of the flames, but I would have been immune to even the sensation of smoke in my lungs and throat.

"So it's true."

"I never said that."

"I know it's true. Emily told me things."

"Like what?" I wanted more wine.

"She said you had about a million bottles of sunscreen, that you were fanatic about using it."

"I have sensitive skin. Besides, I heard that V words can't be out in the sun at all."

"She said you talked about death all the time. And you had clothes, old clothes that fit you perfectly, like they'd been made for you a hundred years ago."

"What can I say? I have a good tailor. This is ridiculous."

"Then once she sipped that wine you kept for yourself. You'd never let her have any; you said it wasn't as good as what you gave her. And it tasted thick and salty and not like wine at all."

"See?" I said. "I was telling the truth. It wasn't as good. It sucks, actually. Not even human blood; it's from cows. I get it from a black market dealer named

Tolstoy, and he knows he can charge me whatever he wants."

Jared jumped to his feet. He looked as if he'd lost weight in the last few days, so that his body seemed to dangle from his broad shoulders like the plastic skeleton decorating my neighbor's door. His face was as pale as mine.

"So it is true!"

"I was just joking." (I wasn't. Tolstoy is a thief, but I hadn't called him since Emily died over a week ago. I had less and less appetite for his contraband now, though I wasn't sure why.)

"Stop acting like this is funny! You are fucked-up."

"So are you."

"That's right. I want you to fuck me up even more."

"That's not an escape. You can never escape this planet that way."

"But it won't matter anymore what happens.

Nothing will matter."

Suddenly I wanted to hold him in my arms, comfort him like a child. I wanted to share my secret. It had been hard to hide it for so long.

Instead, I pushed him away with my words. "Just admit it. You want the power, don't you? What you think is power. It's not. And it's not true that things stop mattering. That's the piece you don't hear about. You still care. You still want. You're still lonely. More lonely. And you still weep, or you would weep if you could—you wish you could weep for some relief—when you live long enough to see the planet you once wanted to escape from burning like a patch of grass under a magnifying glass in the sun."

I thought for a moment that he would drop to his knees and beg me. There were tears in his eyes. They weren't hollow anymore. He had come to life, realizing there was one thing left he still wanted now that Emily was gone.

But it wasn't an option.

"I'm sorry, Jared," I said, as softly as I could. "I want to help you, but I can't do that to you. I mean, I wouldn't. If I were one."

I wasn't really lying. I was no longer sure if I was a V word or if it was possible for me to change him at all. Perhaps the story of Mariette and Camille was not just a fairy tale.

Before I could say anything more, Jared turned and fled from my house into the smoky night.

Need

Jared came back to see me the next evening, hunched in my doorway with that black hair hiding his green eyes. My heart surged in my chest, but I feigned calm. Once again, I let him in.

"What do you want? I told you . . ."

"I came for something else."

"Why should I talk to you? You made some terrible accusations."

"I'm sorry, Charlotte."

I hesitated for a moment. "Accepted."

"I want her back," he said, and my heart sank like

the stones Charles and I used to toss into the lake when we were so very young.

I beckoned him to follow me into the kitchen. I poured him wine, this time without asking, and he took the large glass. I sliced fresh tuna into thin strips with the sharp blade of my kitchen knife. I laid the fish out on a plate with ginger and wasabi. Then we went into the garden and sat by the pool where I first swam with Emily. I imagined her stepping out of the water, naked and laughing, so pretty, so in love with Jared Pierce.

He didn't eat with me, but he drank his wine, and I filled a second glass for him. In the distance we could see the fires flaring along the horizon like a second sunset, like the devil's barbecue.

"Are you coming back to school?" he asked me.

"I don't think so. I'm sick of it, anyway."

"Why did you go at all?"

"It was a lark. I wanted to see what it was like for all of you."

"That's how I feel," he said. "I want to understand you. How it works. What you are."

"Why?"

"Since Emily . . . I started thinking about death. And how to escape it. If there had been a way for her to escape it. You have the answer."

"How do you know?"

"I see that you do. I see it in you. But I want to understand it better." He paused, and I saw his mouth twitch with concentration. "I want to paint you."

And then he had me.

I wanted to be seen the way he had seen Emily in those portraits he did of her. Not as a body but as a soul. Jared could do that. But maybe only with someone he loved. Maybe I would only look like the monster I was inside.

We sat in silence for a while. It was as if this subject he had broached had frightened both of us but also linked us somehow, like some kind of oath sealed in blood. After the sun set, we went into the house.

Jared went out to his car and came back with a sketch pad. I sat on the red sofa with my feet tucked under me, the way Emily always sat, and stared at him.

"Take your hair down," he said.

I reached up and undid the tortoiseshell pins. My hair tumbled over my shoulders.

"Do you think you can understand things by drawing them?" I asked him.

"Yes. If you really look."

"Tell me what you can understand from looking at me."

He paused for a moment. "You are beautiful, that's the first thing. It's almost too much. It keeps most people from seeing anything beyond that. It's the perfect disguise for you. It blinds us. But you're more than that."

He was squinting at my mouth, dashing lines on the page.

"You are incredibly lonely. That's why your eyes look so hungry, and your mouth, it's almost . . . what's the word? . . . depraved, the way your lip droops."

I flinched a little under his gaze.

"You aren't just hungry in a bloodthirsty way. You're hungry for something inside. And you look young, but you move like someone tired who doesn't want to be here, who's trapped in this graceful body but isn't graceful anymore."

It was hard for me to sit so still, hearing those words, feeling those eyes. He kept sketching.

"You're savage. But there's another part of you that's really sweet. And that's the problem. . . ."

He didn't stop sketching. With every mark he made on the page then, I felt a scratch on my skin. There was nothing I could say in reply to his words.

"Am I right?"

"I can't decide if you are cruel or the kindest person I've ever met."

"How is that kind?" he said, but his voice was soft.

"Everyone wants to be seen and understood."

"Emily understood me," he said. "She was the only one."

"You are lucky," I told him. "I couldn't let her get that close to me. I wanted to protect her from that understanding."

"You don't need to protect me," he said. "I've never needed protection."

"I see that. Never before. Now you do."

"You don't know anything about me."

"I do, actually. I can tell a lot by looking, too. I've been observing things for a long time."

"Okay. Go ahead. Tell me."

I closed my eyes. I saw a little boy with black hair and catlike eyes sitting at a table with a family of blonds. They were all laughing, and he wasn't. There was a little blond girl next to him. She took the last roll out and handed him the basket, empty, shrugging her shoulders and smirking.

"Stupid pig," he said.

The man at the head of the table stood up, grabbed

the boy, and dragged him away. The boy was crying and screaming, "I'm sorry! I'm sorry!"

I could see the visions of Jared just as I had been able to see my Charles, the boy I had loved most. It seemed as if these visions were reserved for only my most potent relationships, and they were returning.

"You felt left out when you were growing up," I said. "The outsider. The black sheep. You still are. You lost your real family just as I lost mine. You want revenge. Even being here with me now feels like revenge."

Jared was quiet. I knew I was right.

I kept talking. My eyes were still closed. "You started painting because it was the only way to feel all right. Painting and playing guitar and writing songs. And then you met Emily."

I saw Jared and Emily lying on her bed. Her virginal twin bed with the stuffed animals on it. Purple bears and pink unicorns and lambs with wings. Jared's body was long and lean, wrapped around her from behind.

His hands were on her breasts. Her head was thrust back to reach his mouth.

I opened my eyes.

"You know a lot about me," he said. "Tell me something else about you, to make it fair."

I surprised myself with the words I spoke next. "I've wanted a baby for a long time," I said. "But I thought it was impossible."

"You want a baby? That's one thing I couldn't see."

Jared looked into my eyes. He didn't seem shocked. He didn't look as if he might run away. From my years of experience, I think that, as a general rule, babies frighten young men much more than vampires.

"Take off your shirt," he said.

I looked down at my chiffon blouse. My breasts were tingling with an unfamiliar sensation. I unbuttoned the tiny pearls and took off the blouse to reveal my ivory lace bra. The tingling in my nipples intensified. I hadn't felt this for years.

"Take off your bra." He was looking in my eyes now, harder, as if challenging me not to look away.

I met his gaze defiantly, reached around, and unhooked the bra. My breasts fell out, full and pale, a little too big, out of proportion to my narrow rib cage and waist.

"You loved Emily more than anyone. Because you never felt loved by your parents, you thought it was impossible for you to feel any kind of love for anyone at all. Let alone this much love for one small girl on a bed covered with stuffed toys."

Jared lowered his eyes and kept sketching. I noticed that his hands were shaking. He worked for a long time, more slowly than before. The night seemed to be gathering itself around us like clouds of black smoke. After a while he stood up and walked over to me. He showed me what he had made.

The portrait looked exactly like me. But not as I thought of myself looking now. In Jared's picture I was the girl who had cantered through the fields with her twin brother and collapsed with him by the fireplace at twilight, cheeks flushed and love flickering in her eyes.

Jared fell to his knees before me.

"Please, Char," he whispered. His voice was hoarse. "This isn't only about Emily. Or wanting to escape."

"What is it, then?"

He took my hand, but not to examine it this time. He pressed my open palm to his chest.

"It's about you."

"But you loved Emily."

With his other hand, Jared reached up and stroked my face. I closed my eyes and turned my cheek into his hand. It fit perfectly there. I felt as if he were cradling a fragile shell.

"I did love her," he said. "And I tried not to think about you, but I couldn't help myself. I wanted you from the first time I saw you. Didn't you know that?"

I pulled away from him as if he had scratched me.

"Why? Because of my tits? Because of my hair? I'm sick of all you boys thinking beauty is the only thing."

"No. It wasn't how you look. Emily was beautiful, even though she didn't believe it. You're way too much."

"Thanks."

"You know what I mean. The reason I wanted you . . . it was all the things you've been through. I could see them in your face even though it's so pretty. A century of things. I want to get inside. I want to understand them."

He sat beside me on the couch and ran the back of his hand up and down my arm. It was as if every hair that stood up was a tiny bolt of electricity.

"I want you to teach me."

I lowered my eyes. I remembered how he had watched me when we were with Emily. It wasn't lust in his eyes. It was something else, this thing he spoke of. The artist's desire to see beneath the surface, to understand the shadow and the light.

I had felt guilty at the time, as much as I wanted that look from him. And now Emily was gone forever and the look was all mine. What I felt now was worse than mild guilt; it was a sense of sharp betrayal.

Forgive me, Emily.

Jared said, "I'm more like you than you think. You said it yourself—we both lost our families. We both see too much. We both want to see too much."

I turned to Jared. I could no longer resist.

"I will not pierce your neck like a barbarian," I said. "I will not let you drink from my cut wrist. But my body senses your need, like a mother with a new-born."

"Will it make me one of you?"

I was no longer able to deny what I was to Jared, or at least what I had been.

"No. But it will make you one with me for one night."

Dark Soul

I woke late the next morning, my body drugged with sensation. Jared gazed at me with heavy-lidded eyes. He was so naked under my soft white sheets. I could smell the fragrant mix of our bodies, creating their own perfume. I'd read that perfume has three layers—the top notes that you smell first, the heart notes and the base notes. In Jared's arms I became the evanescent sweetness of lilies. Jared was the heart—sandalwood and cedar. Together we were the animalic musk base. I ran my hands over my body and smelled my fingers. I had a scent again. I would no longer need to imitate the smell of a woman with musk and civet.

I wanted to say to Jared, "I'm alive," but I couldn't speak about it. It was all too much. I now knew what Emily must have felt when she said meeting him had saved her life. But it hadn't ultimately, had it?

Jared had a faraway look in his cat eyes. I remembered the framed picture of Emily on my night table. Part of me wished I had moved it while we made love.

"Are you thinking about her?" I asked, pressing my face into his armpit.

"Why would she do that to herself, Char? I thought she was happy."

"She was happy. She loved you so much. You made her happy."

"But then why?"

"Did she ever tell you what happened? With her mother's boyfriend?"

He nodded and shut his eyes for a moment, as if he

were trying to keep the images out.

Suddenly the room felt too small to hold us—claustrophobic, like a coffin. I couldn't breathe, surrounded by all these old things. The dust motes jumped in a beam of sunlight.

"Jared," I said, "we need to get outside, out of this house."

He heard my urgency; maybe he felt it himself. We didn't stop to shower or eat. He put on the black T-shirt and jeans he'd worn the night before. I wore a white button-down shirt and blue-jean cutoffs with old black cowboy boots decorated with blue and white moons, stars and roses. The pockets of the jeans stuck out beneath the bottom of my shorts. I put my hair in two braids under a straw cowboy hat. We still smelled of each other. I took his hand, and we ran out to my Porsche, got in, and drove along the coast. The winds had died down for a moment, but you could still smell the fires. I didn't care if my house and all my treasures burned while we were gone.

We went east toward Hollywood, away from the burned smell in the air. We went to the flea market in the parking lot at Fairfax and Melrose, where kids were shopping for Halloween costumes. We found Jared a pair of beat-up cowboy boots like mine and laughed at the boys and girls in capes and plastic fangs. We stopped at Johnny Rockets diner and had hamburgers, fries and milk shakes at the shiny chrome counter. I glimpsed our reflections in a shop window. We were a good-looking couple, tall, with our contrasting hair, our big hands, our high cheekbones. For a moment I thought of Charles. If he were here now, he would have dressed like Jared. He would have walked like him, too. I flashed on Jared's naked body from the night before. His broad shoulders, long torso, long legs, lean, hard musculature. Charles had been only two years younger than Jared was now when he died so long ago.

Jared and I walked on Hollywood Boulevard. We saw *Across the Universe* and shared a popcorn and a

Coke. I used my cell phone to take photographs of him standing on Marilyn Monroe's star and James Dean's star.

Jared asked softly, "Can I photograph you? I mean . . . will it work?" and I laughed out loud.

"You mean you didn't check me out in the yearbook or online?"

Then he was embarrassed, and I kissed his cheek. He turned to face me and caught my wrists. He held the camera up above us and snapped it while his lips were on mine. In the picture we just looked like light.

"See?" he said. "You can't photograph. Not because of anything sinister. Because you're too magical to be captured that way."

I said, "No, it's your light. You blinded the camera with all that light coming off you."

"Light?" he said. "No way. I'm a dark soul. But what I really want to know is, who are you?"

The Questions

That night Jared and I drove to the beach. We spread out towels and sat on the sand, looking out at the horizon as the sun fell slowly into the sea.

"What were you like when you were human?"

"A girl."

"How old are you?"

"Never ask a lady her age. It's rude."

"Sorry."

"Accepted."

"What were your parents like?"

"Refined, intellectual, creative, a bit remote."

"What happened to them?"

"They died. In an accident. A long time ago. Fortunately, long enough not to understand what had happened to me."

"Do you miss being human?"

"Yes. Terribly. And yet I fear it after so long."

"How can you live in the light?"

"That is a myth."

"Mirrors?"

"A myth. I have a reflection. But I dislike mirrors."

"Why?"

"The mythology is powerful. It makes me tense. I'm always surprised when I see anything there at all."

"But do you like what you see?"

"No. It doesn't feel like me."

"What would?"

"I suppose a girl with duller skin and hair who looks like she is about to turn eighteen. My eyes look a hundred years old."

"So you still eat human food?"

"I still eat the food I ate when I was like you. Blood tastes good, or it did, but is not the only way to survive."

"Crosses?"

"They give me a queer feeling, but they can't hurt me. I think some of them are pretty. I'd like to wear one as a necklace—a big one, ornate—but that seems like taunting fate."

"Stakes?"

"I don't know. I am not brave enough to find out."

"Who made you?"

"William."

"Why did he do it?"

"He loved me. As much as one of us can love, but maybe that isn't the right word for it."

"Did you love him?"

"I believed I did. I needed him, I thought. I was grief-stricken."

"Why?"

"I had lost my twin brother."

Jared hesitated, then covered my hand with his. "Oh, I'm so sorry. How old were you?"

"Fifteen."

I lowered my head. Why did I still feel it after so long? Suddenly I felt it more than I had since it had happened. Jared's voice was lower when he spoke again.

"What was his name?"

"Charles."

"What was he like?"

"Like me before I was changed, but sweeter and taller, with black hair."

"How did he die?"

"Rheumatic fever."

"What did you do?"

"I wept. I wept until I was as dry as an old woman. Then I let William Eliot find me."

"Eliot? *Mr.* Eliot?"

"Yes. You are a quick study."

"That's why he's here? For you?"

"I don't know why he is here."

"That's why you left school?"

"Yes."

"Will he change me?"

"Don't even speak of it. Stay away from him, Jared."

"I can't. I'm in his English class."

"Stay away!"

"You didn't."

"I do now. And I was vulnerable because of my . . ."

He moved his hand away. "What? Your grief? Unlike me, that is! What about my grief? What about Emily?"

"It is not the solution, believe me. Then you have to live without her forever. It's much worse."

"But do you feel loss the same way? After the change, did you feel loss the same?"

"Oh, no, darling boy. I felt loss more than ever

before. I feel an eternity of loss from which I cannot escape or relieve with tears, because we cannot cry."

"But you're crying now. Your face is wet."

I put my fingers to my cheeks. He was right. They were damp with tears. I had not cried since my change. How could this be?

The sun had disappeared by now. Even the glow along the horizon was gone. For the first time in almost a century, I regretted, with a bittersweet melancholy, the loss of the day. I knew, at that moment, how much I must be transforming. Not only was I weeping, but I felt a stirring in my throat and chest and deep in my belly. It was a sensation I had felt only once in all these years. And only before I was changed.

I did not understand how or why this was happening, but now I believed that it was. Was the quickening of my pulse fear or the thrill of possibility?

"Charlotte, one last thing."

"Yes?"

"It sounds stupid, but . . ."

"Just ask."

"Can you feel, you know, love?"

"I thought I could. But now I realize that it was not really love but a fierce desire."

Jared put his arms around me from behind, and I leaned back on his chest. I could feel his heartbeat against my spine.

"Will you tell me where you have been all these years since you were made?" he asked. "What you learned? What you saw?"

"Someday. I will write it for you. I will write it down," I said, as the best day came to an end and the sweet night began.

Memories of the Great Cities—for Jared

Rome, 1925

We sit beside the Trevi Fountain in our white suits and sun hats. The sea nymphs frolic. The sun glints off the water as only the Mediterranean sun does—a dazzle of gold like a handful of tossed coins. The fountain is full of coins, full of wishes.

"I can make your every wish come true," William whispers. He has my wrists caught in one hand. His mouth is near my neck. He smells of the gardenia in his buttonhole and nothing else.

Every wish. But he does not know that there is only one wish and that it can never come true. Charles is gone forever.

"Darling," William says, "I have chosen you because I need a companion. And not just any girl could hold my interest for eternity. It will be a difficult task. The world is full of disasters and terrible beauty. But you, my dear, I'm sure you can meet the challenge."

Paris, 1925

We walk along the Rive Gauche. Behind us is the Eiffel Tower, lit up with a sign that reads "Citroën." In front of us is the little crystal tower made by the jeweler and sculptor Lalique, encrusted with 140 tiny figures. The water spilling off the tower glitters in the night. We have visited the Galeries Lafayette studios, all of marble with a sunburst design at the entrance. Everything is soft shades of rose against hard silver and black.

It as if we have entered a fairyland of neon lights,

steel chevrons, bronze sculptures, stone archways, strange gardens. I can't tell if the magic is the place or from the way my vision has changed since William made me.

We are at the *Exposition Internationale des Arts Decoratifs et Industriels Modernes*, witnessing the formal birth of Art Deco, wth its sleek metallic lines, its jewellike faceted surfaces. It is a style of opulence after the austerity of the war, but soon it will become outmoded, considered ostentatious decoration and replaced by purity and function.

I am wearing a dress by Paul Poiret, a celery-green silk crepe sheath beaded with geometric gold and silver, a cloche hat and a gray coat with a fox-fur collar. Poiret, the emperor of fashion, has provided three decorative barges for the exposition, but after this he will fall into financial ruin. No more embellishments—roses everywhere, silver curlicues and swirls, crystal bottles with petal-shaped stoppers. His perfume line, Rosine, named after his daughter, with fragrances called La Rose de Rosine, Pierrot, Fan Fan La Tulipe, Le Fruit Defendu and Nuit de Chine, will disappear from the market. He will die penniless in 1944, as out of fashion as the charming buildings all around us.

William and I will never go out of fashion. He will teach me. I will learn to adapt, to be always relevant. It is part of our trick.

William holds my kid-gloved hand in his. He seems aware of every slight gesture I make, inquiring whether I need refreshment or rest. I am his little fledgling, relying totally on him for all my needs now.

A boy passes us, a tall boy with black hair, wearing a pale coat.

William's glance flickers across my face.

"Are you all right?"

He knows I am thinking of Charles. But I feel so different now. I feel strangely light in a lovely way, but also empty. Too empty, perhaps. I touch my cheeks. They are dry of tears. Before I changed, my skin was not this smooth, this poreless—white china. Sometimes it broke out in small red spots. My eyes were not this dry. But luckily we are in Paris. The city glitters around me like a huge jewelry box, like a thousand candlelit perfume bottles on black velvet, and I pretend the shine is due to the reflection of my imaginary tears.

"Yes," I say. "I am all right, William, although I hardly know the meaning of the words." All right for whom? For what?

A few days later, we receive a telegram.

I stare at the paper in my hand.

Regret to inform you. Stop. Carl and Christine Elizabeth Emerson. Stop. Death in automobile crash. Stop. Return at once. Stop. Condolences. Stop.

Stop stop stop.

I look at William. He is watching me closely. The paper in my hands does not tremble.

"We will go immediately," he says.

When William and I return home for the funeral, I wear a black veil over my face, not to hide the tears but to hide the fact that there are none.

I think of how, before Charles died, my father would let me come up the tower to watch the stars. He told me all the names of the planets and constellations.

He said, "The ancient gods haven't left us. They are just waiting up there, waiting to return when they are most needed."

"Will I ever see them return?" I asked when I was six. "I want to meet Venus!"

"No, Charlotte. I believe it will be many lifetimes from now, when our planet is in great danger. In our lifetime the planet will still be safe."

He had no idea that his only daughter might live to see the planet in such danger, in such need of divine intervention from Mars and Venus, Jupiter and Neptune.

My mother dressed me up as Venus once. She made

me a wreath of purple Jacob's ladder and mountain laurel. She sewed me a robe of purple velvet. Charles was young enough then to let her dress him up as Mars, in a toga and laurel wreath. He liked the cut-out bow and arrow our mother made him. She played her harp, and I danced, and Charles ran through the house sounding his war cries.

I think about the fact that I left her when she could hardly rise from her bed, hardly feed herself, so that I could go to Europe and become a monster.

There is only one consolation. I am a little relieved, standing in the cemetery in my veil in the rain, that my mother and father did not have to live to experience the loss of both their children. Although I am here in body, I realize that the Charlotte they birthed and raised and loved is gone. A pretty monster—who would have frightened her parents because she never aged past seventeen, a creature who has no tears for them, for anyone—stands in her place.

✳ ✳ ✳

Manhattan, 1925

After my parents' funeral, William takes me to New York City. I am wearing the latest fashions from Paris—a Chanel cardigan that William bought for me, Chanel No. 5 perfume to cover up my uncanny scentlessness. We stay at the Plaza Hotel, a building designed after a huge French chateau, with a statue of Pomona, Roman goddess of the orchards, in the fountain. Our suite is decorated in white and gold. The bathroom floor is inlaid with mosaic tile. Baccarat crystal chandeliers light the lobby. We dine at the Palm Court on damask-covered chairs, under a stained-glass ceiling, at white linen and crystal covered tables.

Sometimes I sit at a table with a candle burning before me and try to write the way I did before William came. I want Charles to come back to me through the words, but he never does. It is as if my ability to create has been spirited away with this new life. I go to my room and look at myself in the gold-framed mirror. The flawlessness and perfect pallor of my skin still fascinates me. I still check my undergarments for blood every few weeks, but I have ceased to bleed. The implications of this have not fully dawned on me yet, or perhaps I am too young still to really care. I had never thought of having children before. I didn't want to be tied down like that. I had imagined some prolonged childhood, scampering unfettered through meadows with my brother at my side.

Now the only blood I see will be the blood William brings me to drink, disguised as wine.

At first he hid it from me. How he got this blood. And I never asked; I didn't want to know. But slowly, in those first months of my change, he began to use me to help him procure the thing we needed.

Unsuspecting young men and women visit museums with us in the day, ride with us in carriages through the park at night, dine with us in glittering rooms, and, drunk on our wine, fall asleep like babies with their heads on our pillows.

We will live like this for years to come, and every time I balk, every time I tell him I have had enough, he takes me in his arms and kisses me, gives me jewels and flowers, shoes and perfume.

"I regret this part, too, Charlotte. But there is no other way. We must make the best of it. We must love our victims, honor and respect them. We give them meaning. We give them value. By dying this way, their lives have purpose."

He makes me believe that we are only being true to our natures, nothing more.

San Francisco, 1939

Fourteen years have passed since William made me. I've been his creature almost as long as I was human, and in no time I'll have left my young human self far behind. Not just chronologically; I am less and less like the girl I was. I don't think about my parents much, or even Charles, except in those moments when someone who resembles him crosses my path. I am a devoted partner to William, and my concerns revolve around keeping him happy as well as experiencing all the cultural riches he offers me. But I am already growing restless.

William was here in San Francisco in 1915 for the Panama-Pacific International Exhibition. He has told me about the Tower of Jewels, 435 feet covered in 100,000 glass gems lighting up the night. The Tower of Jewels was temporary, but the Palace of Fine Arts is still there, with its dome, its colonnade, its frieze of weeping women reflected in the water that surrounds it. Swans float on the still surface, and the sky is soft and gray, with very little threat of sun. To brighten things dangerously, I wear a shocking-pink Elsa Schiaparelli dress with silver tambourine buttons.

William likes to travel to see the world's marvels, to appreciate the beauty of man's artistic achievements. He says they inspire him.

Now we are on Treasure Island for the new

exhibition, held boldly in the wake of the Great Depression. Two bridges have been built, and an exposition is being held defiantly, as if to say, "This city is immune from such calamity." Just as the 1915 world's fair was held only a few years after an earthquake that nearly ruined San Francisco forever.

In this way, the bold but foggy city reminds me of myself and William. Laughing in the face of danger. Challenged by it to grow bigger, more powerful, more immune.

William has things to show me. The Court of Flowers. The Elephant Tower. The Peru Building. The Tower of the Sun.

"Look! Look!" he says. "Aren't humans endearing? I can hardly remember what it was like to be one anymore. They make magical little structures to boast about how ingenious they are. They make a whole temporary city just to boast."

"At least they make something," I say.

I am angry at William today. I used to be so

creative; perhaps I could have been a painter or a writer. He took that away. I am tired of his incessant talk, his cold eyes. Last night I had to lure a young couple to him again. He made me watch but I refused to eat. I went hungry. Now I am weak.

"I make things, too," William says haughtily. He stops and takes my face in his hands. "I made the prettiest thing of all. And she isn't going to be destroyed by earthquakes or wars. She'll eat all her dinner tonight like a good girl. She is going to live forever."

When you become only art and not the artist, the girl in the shocking-pink dress, what becomes of your soul?

London, 1940

Now I only wear a brown gabardine suit. In Paris, in defiance, the women are wearing high heels, full skirts, and even fur coats. They say the enemy will have less fabric if they use more.

When the bombing started, most everyone went underground, but William, impervious, takes my hand and leads me up to a high balcony where we can survey a large portion of the city.

"It's beautiful, isn't it?" he murmurs.

I must look horrified, because he puts his arm around my waist. "Oh, I know, it's evil personified, but you can't deny that it is beautiful, too. And I hate to say it, but bloodshed fosters the creative spirit. They are connected."

There are too many fires to count. The horizon is aflame, like a hundred suns flaring before they set. But these suns do not set. They keep raging, consuming the city in red flashes and, above that, billows of pink smoke. The buzzing sound of the planes' motors seemed to emanate from the fires themselves, as if the flames are made up of thousands of burning bees. From where we stand we can see the Thames and the dome of St. Paul's Cathedral, both glowing surreally. This is the first time in my life, as a human or something else, that I contemplate an apocalypse.

"What will we do if the world ends?" I ask William, as all around us the city burns to ash beneath a sky of terrible roses.

"We will wander the ruins together," he tells me.

Then we put on the tin hats he's made for us and takes my hand. We run down, down, down the staircases to cavort and dance in hell.

Hiroshima, 1945

When we arrive, it hasn't happened yet.

The city fills a valley between hills and sea. Later I will find out that this was one reason it was chosen. To focus the destruction in one area. I don't know why he wanted to come.

"Why?" I asked when he mentioned it. "The war is on. I've had enough."

"I know," he said. "But remember that wars feed . . ."

"Culture and creativity. I know, you've told me."

"And?"

"I don't see that at all. They just bring death."

But I came with him anyway. Maybe part of me believed that seeing the horrors might wake me up again, in some way bring back my humanity.

I was wrong. The horror hadn't even really begun. That much horror can kill even the soul of a soulless being.

We are staying at a traditional *ryokan*, or hotel, in the outskirts. We sit on tatami mats; eat fish and rice; wear kimonos covered with peonies, pine trees, cranes. It is possible to pretend the world is peaceful. Until that day.

From the *ryokan* we see the flash of light, the sky with its mushroom cloud. A death's-head in the sky. Black smoke. A whole city vanishing in a moment. If we were human we would have lost our hair later, developed tumors, died from the radiation. But our immortality saves us again.

They say that light patterns on clothing protected one's skin and black patterns were imprinted onto the skin from the flash.

Soon after this disaster, in a hotel room in Paris,

William rips up one of the kimonos he'd bought me in Japan. It has large dark flowers on a pale ground. I imagine flower scars, big petals burned into my skin. He lays me on the bed and ties my wrists and ankles with the strips of silk.

"Call me master," he says.

"Tatsujin."

He holds a candle over me and drips wax on my breasts and belly. The wax is scalding but cools immediately, turns powder soft. Of course I don't feel a bit of pain. I don't cry. Maybe he is trying to punish me, or maybe he is trying to save me with my own tears. But of course none come.

I think about the London bombing, and now this. I wonder if somehow William attracts disaster to him wherever he goes.

Hollywood, 1947

William is called Billy now. He has come here to be an actor and, he says, to help us forget some of the horrors we have seen. Acting seems to be a good way to forget a lot of things. But it's hard to forget the image of the Black Dahlia, Elizabeth Short, with her blue eyes and black locks. And the other images, the pictures they took in the morgue where she doesn't look like a person at all but a chopped-up thing. It even sickens monsters like us.

Billy looks debonair with his brilliantined hair, his sharkskin suits, two-toned oxford shoes. We go out for martinis and dancing at the Trocadero or Perino's. Sometimes we catch a glimpse of a movie star. They look like us—too pretty, too smooth. Billy wants a girl and a boy this time, aspiring actors maybe. I find a couple sitting at a pale pink booth. I'm wearing a sky-blue chiffon dress and ankle-strap shoes, my hair in a bun with loose tendrils. I smile at them and remove my white glove to take their hands. They join us for a cocktail. Music plays, a Nat King Cole song, and the lighting is rosy. Potted palms all around, parquet floors. So elegant. The girl is a brunette in a dove-gray dress and the boy is blond with a Midwestern accent.

Billy leans over to me and whispers in my ear. "You did well, Char. Very pretty. Both."

He sees a flash of rebellion mixed with fear in my eyes and adds, "It's just two little lives. We've been through wars, darling."

"What?" the girl asks. "What did you say?"

"We were just saying how lovely it is to be here celebrating after all the hard times we've seen."

He raises his glass to the pretty prey with their trusting martini eyes. "Cheers," he says hoarsely. "To eternal life."

The couple giggle and clink their glasses, not knowing they salute their death.

Bethel, 1969 (Woodstock)

So many years of the same thing. Wandering. Seduction. Death. Only the scenery, clothing and faces change. Except for our faces. They always stay the same.

I sit in the rain. It streams over me, soaking my

hair and my dress so that my breasts show through the thin, tie-dyed fabric. Rainwater fills my eyes and I pretend I am crying. Ravi Shankar is playing on the stage. Graceful rhythms of the tabla are stirring something ancient and human in my heart, but my tears are still only rain.

Three people will die here. A heroin overdose. A ruptured appendix. The man who was run over by a tractor in his sleep.

Don't think about the three deaths.

When William heard about them, he said, "Sacrifice to the gods, I suppose."

If I could still shiver, I would. Billy isn't afraid of horror, but I am; maybe therein lies my salvation.

A woman gave birth in the back of a pickup truck. I could hear her screams. I wonder what it would be like to hold my own baby in my arms. The small, round, wet head against my breast—this is something I will never know. It is another thing Billy has taken from me, but I try never to think of it. By now, if he had not made me, I would be an old woman, too old for babies, maybe no longer beautiful. If I ever accused him of robbing me of the gift of life, he would point this out. He would say, "I have given you the greatest gift of life there is."

I look around for Billy, but he is gone. Muddy half-dressed girls and boys dance around me. I think, *How can it be that the world changes so much all the time?* I feel the deep sense of emptiness that comes from having to witness so much change, over and over again, forever.

The only way I can do it, I think, is to have Billy by my side. At least I will have someone who understands what is like to never grow old, someone who will never leave me. Even though he is savage, even though he is cruel, he is at least immortal. That alone makes him invaluable to me. He must never leave.

Where is he?

I take off my wet dress, peel the fabric away from my body, and stand to dance with the girls and boys in the relentless rain. I have seen bombings. I have

seen brutality. I have seen blood. What is this? A bac-
chanal, a joyous thing, a brief interlude of peace and
love. A time that will never come again. *Celebrate the
rain, the mud, Charlotte,* I tell myself. *Celebrate the lovely bare
flesh, beating beneath the surface with young blood.*

*Maybe someday you, too, can leave the earth with this memory
inside you.*

I wonder, if so much of the mythology about us
is untrue, what of the myth of the stake through the
heart? Is that true? Who would do such a thing for
me? Who would ever love me that much?

London, 1972

If not by disasters and music, I mostly remember my
history by what I wore.

Now it is floppy suede hats, minidresses, and psy-
chedelic tights or bell-bottoms, purple suede platform
boots. My eyelashes are false and sparkled. My lips
are Mary Quant white. Billy in his three-piece dandy
suits with the flared legs, thick-heeled boots. His hair

brushes his collar, and he sports a handlebar mustache.

We live in a Victorian flat with garlands embossed on the ceilings and walls. I remember the flat by closing my eyes and seeing myself dressed in my Carnaby Street finery, dancing around the living room to the Rolling Stones. "Wild Horses." That's how I feel about Billy; nothing can drag me away from him. His favorite Stones song is "Sympathy for the Devil."

There are always people crashed out on our floor; you have to step over bodies in the morning to get to the kitchen. Some of the girls are the ones I have procured for Billy, lost souls with pretty hair, long legs and lashes whom I found at boutiques or bars or in dark alleys. I feel bad every time I bring one home, but I can't seem to stop. I am like a loyal hunting dog dragging back the birds by their broken necks. But these birds have not been shot down yet; that is to come.

Why do I keep doing it? Not only because it is my nature. Not only because I am devoted and afraid. I realize now that my participation in his work was the closest I could get to creating something when I had nothing left to make myself.

Paris, 1976

Sometimes Billy takes me with him when he goes out. We walk along the Champs Élysées at night. He is incensed by the McDonald's they've put there, can't seem to get over it.

"And they think because they serve red wine it is all right! *Merde!*"

In France, Billy wants me to dress elegantly and all in black. I have a collection of black dresses and a lot of colorful printed silk scarves.

"They can make it seem that you have more clothes," he tells as he gives me a new Hermès scarf as a present.

I have my original black Chanel cardigan from the

1920s and Coco's No. 5 perfume. Billy prefers classic fashion for me, though he is quite a dandy himself, and I am still trying to please him.

I really want to eat at McDonald's and to buy one of the plastic necklaces full of virulent-seeming glow-in-the-dark green liquid that vendors sell along the boulevard, but Billy says they look cheap and are only for tourists.

The city stretches out before us, twinkling with the magic of so many lovers' fantasies and dreams. It has changed so much since Billy first brought me here. The fast food, the plastic, the traffic. But then, I've changed, too. He and I have changed. Once we loved each other all night long. He whispered poetry into my ear. He told me he would love me forever. Now we are like an old bickering couple, and we do not even have death to look forward to as an escape from each other.

Manhattan, 1986

Ten years can be a long time in the world of mortal fashion.

I have my hair teased over the bandana at my brow. Strategically ripped white T-shirts over black spandex tights and shoes with pointed toes. Lots of bangles and chains. I want to wear big crosses for the fun, the irony of it, but it feels wrong, weirdly dangerous somehow, though I wouldn't admit it. I am still dancing. The T-shirt, cut at the neck, slips off over my bare shoulders. The bangles click together.

This time I am dancing to Madonna in a penthouse apartment lit with candles. Black marble floors. City shining down below us, looking immune, but it isn't. Six years ago John Lennon was shot. We were here then, at the eye of the storm again. Lennon was only forty years old and as in love as a man can be. I remember how one Halloween Billy and I dressed in white and flowers, and I wore a long black wig, pretending to be Yoko. I suppose Billy thought this costume, like the crosses he wears, was ironic. I didn't tell him that it was my fantasy, the way I believed love was supposed to manifest itself.

But very little looks the way it really is. People are

dying fast and it is blood-related, but it has nothing to do with us.

Billy walks in—dark eye makeup smudged, a long chain in his ear with a cross dangling at the end. His hair is short and bleached, with dark roots, not the teased pompadour I would have expected based on his decadent style from the last decades; he's a little more dignified now. He doesn't like how I am dressed—I can tell by his expression—but I am no longer quite as subservient anymore. I'll wear what I like; it's about the only way I have to express myself.

Billy lies down on the couch and turns on the TV. There aren't any sexy girls or boys lying around on the floor. AIDS has made everyone more cautious, more monogamous. Even though it can't affect us, it's hard to watch these lovely men becoming all eyes and cheekbones, then hooked up in a hospital, driven through streets in hearses, in coffins that will never open.

Once Billy said, "There's something so beautiful

about all these young people becoming aware of their mortality. It's a shame it took this disease to do it, though. But it's still beautiful."

I close my eyes and keep dancing, trying to forget that those words came from the lips of the man who has become my whole life.

Seattle, 1994

Kurt Cobain has just died. And here we are. Eight years later and we're in an entirely new era, but our faces are just as youthful. I am wearing a white satin slip dress, a plaid flannel shirt, torn black leggings and black Converse sneakers, and am sitting curled up in front of the TV, drinking wine. I can't believe Kurt's dead. He looked like me and Charles. He could have been our brother.

They say he shot himself in the head.

Part of me is jealous, although I feel guilty for thinking this.

Outside it is raining. The relentless rain. Why do

we live here? Our apartment is large and sprawling, with bookshelves everywhere, a fireplace and a wall of windows looking out over the wet courtyard garden. Sometimes I walk around the lake and look at the flowering trees. I go to the outdoor market and buy oysters and wine. Sometimes I spend whole days in a bookstore. Mostly I wait and wait for Billy to come home.

He's not back until late that night. I'm still in the chair with the television on. I can't cry, but I want to more than anything. Without tears the pain turns to rage. I want to smash the TV. *Why did you kill yourself? You had everything. Even mortality to save you eventually. What have you left me with? Nothing.*

Manhattan, 2001

Finally the city is quiet. Too quiet. Hardly any sirens anymore. The silence of defeat. And the air still toxic. Photographs of missing family members paper the walls. I am alone in the apartment again, waiting for

William. He's been gone since it happened. I know he is safe, but I'm not sure I am. I've been sitting like this for days with William's black cat, Ezra, on my lap. I haven't eaten, showered, or changed my clothes. I have on the same pair of ripped jeans, the same black cashmere sweater. The television is always on, showing the footage of those planes and the towers over and over again.

At last there is the sound of his key in the door.

The man I share my life with sits beside me. He has started referring to himself as William again, thinks it's more "twenty-first century."

"What's wrong with you?" he asks. "You look like shit."

"I can't do this anymore," I say. "Everywhere I go with you, something horrible happens."

"I know. It's as if I attract it. Maybe you bring it out in me. It's gotten a little out of control now, hasn't it?"

"It's like we're stuck in hell together."

"We are, my darling. We are. But what's the

alternative? Being in hell alone?"

I get up from the couch. Suddenly a rush of anger infuses me with energy. I go into the bedroom and find the Louis Vuitton steamer trunk. I pack it with as many of my vintage clothes as it will hold. (Later I will pay two men to come when William is not there and take the rest.) And then I leave.

Willam just reclines on the sofa, watching me go. He thinks I will be back in no time.

He is wrong.

Los Angeles, 2001–2007

In no time I meet a wealthy gentleman who worships me and gives me everything I desire. All I have to do is accompany him to his premieres and parties and let him fuck me once in a while. I know it sounds bad, but remember, I am a monster. At least I treat him kindly and never drink his blood or the blood of his friends or employees. To be honest, none of their blood smells good to me anyway. I spend my days shopping for treasures. When he dies, he leaves me everything.

The one thing I do not have for all these years is a friend, a companion, someone to share my riches with, someone who is not afraid of the strange girl in the palace of beautiful things. Someone intelligent and beautiful and sweet. Until Emily comes into my life.

I never hear from William Eliot again, but I can also never shake the sensation that someday he will return.

William Stone

It was Halloween, the night after Jared's questions on the beach.

I thought it was another trick-or-treater, and I opened the door. The dry-ice mist rising from the bucket on my porch and the strings of orange jack-o'-lantern lights made the man glow. He wore a hideous mask from one of those disgusting slasher movies and carried some kind of ugly plastic sword.

"Trick or treat," he said. "Or should I say, dark trick, dark treat?"

"You should say nothing," I replied. "You should

go away and never come back."

A group of little goblins with pillowcases full of candy were coming up the path. William stepped back into the shadows while I placated them with sweets and watched them hop off into the night.

Before I could close the door, I felt William's hand on my wrist. His grip was firm and steady. I thought of Jared, with his gentle touch, his tender kisses. I thought of Jared shaking on my red velvet couch. Jared, who would die like all the rest, leaving me alone.

But William would not die. He would be here when the sun burned the earth to a crisp through that growing hole in the sky. We would be in hell together forever.

"Forgive me," he whispered.

And then I let him lead me into my house.

Or perhaps I led him.

He took off the horror-show mask. He tossed away the sword and dropped to his knees on my Oriental carpet. His hands held my hipbones.

"Forgive me," he said again. "I'm sorry I appeared like that, so suddenly, and startled you. I've been searching for so long. When I saw you I experienced all the same sensations I had at the moment of your making."

I turned my back to him and he rose.

"What? Didn't you feel it, too?"

I tensed as he touched my shoulder, touched the hair that fell down my back. Wrapped a lock around the middle of his hand, turned it, wrapped it, tugged so gently but enough that my head went back a tiny bit toward him.

"Why are you here? What do you want?"

"At first I came to take you back."

"Take me back?" I said, turning to face him. My scalp pulled as my hair slipped from his hand. "You will never take me back!"

"But then I changed my mind," he continued. "I have released you. I have given you what you always wanted."

I stepped closer to him, my heart thumping with anger. "What can you give me? The first time you gave me what you thought I wanted, you ruined my life."

I was pounding his chest with my fists, pounding and pounding with the fury of almost a century. And he caught my wrists in his hands and held me steady, held me the way you hold a child out of control with anger until finally they surrender, melting into their sorrow.

"You wanted it, Charlotte. You came to my room in Rome and asked to be changed. You wanted anything that would take away your pain."

"But you did it. You knew that I would suffer more. I was only a girl. You didn't tell me how it would be."

"It is different for us all. And you never asked."

Why had I never asked William Stone Eliot about what it would be like, about how he became what he was? I thought of Jared asking me so many questions, one after another, as if he wanted to crawl inside me.

So curious. But I never wanted to know about William. I was terrified to know.

Now, gripped again by his lifeless white arms but no longer blinded as I had been for so long, I saw visions of who he really was.

I see a boy huddled in the corner of a room, watching a woman who is lying on a bed. Her neck is swollen and her limbs are black. I see the boy in a dark, dirty orphanage, where the cries of children echo through the halls.

In a hospital ward, many of the children are dying.

I see a young man wandering through the streets, thin, gaunt, bearded. I see him sitting on a cot in a garret, woolen socks with the toes cut off worn over his hands like gloves, hands trembling as he scribbles words on paper and then, when he runs out of paper, scribbles the words all over the walls of the room. I see him in a room like a cage, shaking the bars, begging for something with which to write, clawing at himself to get blood from his own body to write with. I see him cast back out onto the street with no money, nowhere to go.

He wants to tell a story. He believes he is an artist; he has stories to tell, but no one will listen to him. No one understands the words he screams in his cell, although to him they are a great epic poem, an aria.

A dark alley. Rats scurrying. A woman in the shadows. She is small, with dark ringlets under her hood, a sweet young face. You would think she would be afraid of him. Instead, as she approaches, he draws back, terrified. She smiles gently, beatific, but her eyes are the eyes of something unspeakable.

"Do not be afraid, William. Have you never seen an angel before?"

"Angel of darkness! I see them all the time in my vile dreams since my mother died! Get away from me."

"Oh, William, do not fear. I can save you from diseases like the one that killed your mother. I have the answers. You are an artist, William. No one understands you. They think you are mad, but you are only a little lost. An artist must learn to feed off the world. That is the only way he can survive. That is the only way he can stop feeding off himself, eating himself alive from within. I can show you how."

I did not believe that this was true. The opposite was true. By becoming artists we monsters can sometimes be redeemed. We can give instead of devouring.

I pulled away from William.

"Get out of here!" I screamed. "I am through with you. Even if I have to live in eternity alone."

I waited for him to protest, but he only smiled, turned, and walked out the door.

A V in Love

After William left, I scrubbed myself in the shower and climbed into bed. I felt dirty, diseased, my skin crawling with the memory of his touch. Why had I let him in at all?

I remembered the way Jared had touched me, the salty taste of his skin, the warm, sweet smell under his arms, the smoothness of his chest and how his back felt undulating over me.

I should never have let William come into my house. All I could think of was Jared. I knew I needed to see him. Maybe if he touched me again I could forget that William had come back.

I texted Jared: i wnt to c u 2nite

He wrote back: 7 pm pik me up

Now that William had come to my door, I no longer felt safer in my house. And being with Jared made me bold.

First we went to a sushi restaurant on Main Street. I spoke Japanese to the sushi chef, bowed and called him *tatsujin,* so he gave us all kinds of special dishes, decorated with leaves and orchids.

"Where'd you learn Japanese?" Jared asked me.

"In the forties, in Japan," I said. And then I stopped eating, thinking of the sickening flash, the cloud mushrooming in the sky.

Tatsujin. William was my master then.

"What's wrong?" Jared asked me. "Are you okay? You look pale."

"We all look pale, remember?" I joked, to change the subject. "There are thousands of teenagers all over the world who try to make themselves pale and dress in black so that they pass for one of us."

"No," Jared said, "you're not always so pale any-more, goth girl." He leaned in closer. "The other night, when I touched you, you lit up."

"Maybe that's what happens when a human loves us," I said. Then I wished I hadn't. But Jared put down his chopsticks. He turned to me and looked into my eyes like he was staring through an entranceway.

"What happens when one of your kind loves one of us, then?" he asked. "Do they make us into one of you?"

"No. If we really love someone, we don't do that. No matter how much we want to."

He went back to eating again. I could tell he was upset.

"We also do this when we are in love," I said. I lifted a piece of *tako* with my chopsticks; the white octopus flesh rimmed with purple suction cups quiv-ered in the air between us, and then I held it to his lips. "We feed," I said.

After dinner, I drove us to the club where Emily and I had danced together. The bouncer led us up to the front of the line after one glance at my gold Dolce & Gabbana minidress and gladiator platforms. I took Jared's hand as we walked inside.

"I came here with Emily," I said into his ear.

He nodded, looking around the room as if he were searching for her in the crowd.

"I keep thinking I'm going to see her," he shouted at me over the music.

"I know. Me, too."

I led him to a corner, where we could hear each other better. We stood close together, almost touching but not quite. His eyes looked haunted. I wanted to be her for him, take away the sorrow.

"You miss her a lot, don't you?"

"Yes. But when I think about it I feel guilty, because if she were here I wouldn't know what to do."

"Why?"

"You know why."

"Say it."

"I think I'm falling in love with you, too."

We looked at each other for a moment. The lights of the club scattered us with rainbows.

"This is something else we do when we are in love," I said.

"What?"

"We dance. We remember what it felt like to be human and dance."

I took his hand. Jared's body moved gracefully next to mine. His eyes never strayed from my face. He put his hand on my lower back and I felt my knees weaken, a dampness between my legs. I leaned in close.

"There is another thing we remember," I said into his ear, loud enough that he could hear above the pounding music. I put his hand on my taut thigh. It was so dark and we were so close that I could ease his hand up to my hip and across my lower belly with no one noticing, dip him into me for a second so his fingers felt the warmth, the downy wetness and then the parting.

The Artist Is a V Word

Look at van Gogh. Look at Sylvia Plath. Anne Sexton. Virginia Woolf. Diane Arbus. They are the ones I admire. But what is the theme here? These artists, like all artists, being true to their natures, fed off the world. They wanted to suck it dry. Instead, they killed themselves. Now look at Picasso. He fed off the world, whole chunks of it broken off and stuck on canvas, but he felt no guilt. He survived. It is not that much different with us. Some of us, like William

Stone Eliot, feed happily off the world. Others of us suffer for our needs.

What kind of monster would you be?

What kind of artist might I become?

And if I became an artist now, might I realize that art is really nothing like vampirism? It gives as much as it takes. It might ultimately be the way I could survive.

I used to paint and draw, play the violin and the piano. I used to sing. That was when I was a living girl. I used to record my thoughts in a journal. I wanted to tell stories about myself and Charles and share them with the world. I wanted to consume the beauty, but then it became too much for me to contain inside my body.

When I was changed, I had no stories I wanted to tell. I stopped for many years. I grew impetuous and fiendish. After I left William, I thought it would get better, but I was even more empty. I no longer even had the dark story of my master, only my own loneliness. What became important was studying the groups of children at the high school, how they distinguished themselves with their clothes and their hair, how they sat together in packs the way animals do. I came to high school because I was bored, frankly. I would travel again someday, but it felt too tiring to do so now.

Now there were boys to look at. I could tell what they would grow up into. Most would became better-looking; a few, perhaps the early bloomers, the popular ones, worse. I was interested in the patterns of their acne, especially the really bad cases. I sniffed the air as they walked by, under the weight of their backpacks, hooked up to their iPods, their cell phones. I could distinguish sweat, mildewy socks and jerseys, marijuana, French fries, cologne. Occasionally I found one interesting enough to wonder what he would be like immortalized that way, with his lips still in that sensual, jutting stage, his pimples and his loping stride. Though the pimples would no doubt vanish, and how happy he would be with immortality and flawless skin! At least at first.

I studied shoes in magazines and online, fascinated by each trend, though I had seen most of it before. Platforms with carved wedges. Two-toned satin sandals. High-heeled lace-up oxfords. Dove-gray pointed-toe miniboots. I bought them all. I downloaded songs. And finally, after Emily's death, I began writing again, just as I did when I was human. These words you see before you. I wrote more after Jared held me in his arms. At least this is something. At least this is a way to get back a little to who I once was.

The Girl in the
Red Dress

All I wanted to do was to forget about William, but it was not so easy.

Jared and I went to the Los Angeles County Museum to look at the Rodin sculptures. The air smelled of tar from the pits of inky black stuff bubbling up from the lawn. We held hands and wandered along the winding paths, among the statues of prehistoric animals. The day was overcast but warm, and I wore a silk Pucci sundress and Christian Louboutin sandals. Jared had on his usual jeans and was carrying his sketchbook. He said he liked to sketch from sculptures because the forms were so clear and solid.

In the museum the Danaïd lay on her side, with her bony back and her hair covering her face as if she were grieving, transforming into water, the marble liquid as a river. Saint John the Baptist's severed head. A pianist's hand. The female faun kneeling, her face long and animalic. The old woman who had once been a great beauty. The man on his knees before his naked idol. I told Jared that I had seen these sculptures in the museum in Paris—the Hôtel Biron, where Rodin had rented space to work. It was a mansion with tall glass windows and bright rooms surrounded by the now carefully landscaped, once wild, gardens where Rodin had entertained his guests. I told Jared about Rodin's young mistress and model, the blue-eyed sculptor Camille Claudel, and how she had gone mad and died in an asylum. We talked about the way artists had suffered and changed their pain into beauty. How it saved some but not others. Jared sat on a bench and sketched the Danaïd while I wandered through the museum, imagining how someday he would exhibit his paintings of me at galleries all around the world. I only hoped I would fade with him before the paintings did.

The next day we looked at crumbling marble antiquities at the Getty Villa on a hill above the Pacific Ocean.

"This reminds me of your house," Jared said, as we walked along the Corinthian colonnade beside a mural of garlands and trompe l'œil architecture.

"I knew you were just spending time with me because of my house."

He stopped and looked at me. The sun was shining off the rectangular pool. The blackened bronze sculptures with their eerie inlaid white eyes glowed as if they were lit from within. I had taken off my sun hat; the light didn't make me feel afraid.

"I'd be with you if you lived in a one-room apartment," he said.

In a tiny, darkened hallway full of small, erotic drawings and sculptures—a priapic centaur chasing a nymph, a faun copulating with a she-goat—he ran his hand along the back waistband of my jeans and I shivered so that tiny bumps rose up.

On other mornings we sat on the outdoor patio at the Urth Caffé in Santa Monica, and Jared sketched and I wrote. We ate poached eggs and spinach wrapped in salmon on brioches and blackout chocolate cake, and drank green-tea lattes the color of milky jade. I had stopped calling Tolstoy entirely. I no longer drank the blood he sold; it made me vomit now. For the following few days and nights, though, I still preferred my meat rare.

Jared and I got takeout food and ate it out of the containers with our fingers by my pool. We made each other CDs and lit hundreds of candles and made love for hours. I dressed up for him in my costumes of various eras and pretended to be Camille Claudel, Coco Chanel, Marilyn Monroe, Edie Sedgwick, Madonna, Gisele, Kate Moss.

"I like you as you the most," he said, taking off my platinum-blond wig and slowly unlacing the black leather corset that pushed my breasts up over the top.

One night he didn't come. The candles were burning down to nothing, the ice in the champagne bucket had melted and I had listened to the same old Bowie CD over and over again. I called him and texted, but he didn't respond. Something felt wrong in my bones. That was when I got in my car and drove to the house in Venice. The house William and I had abandoned years before, when we moved to the Northeast.

I don't know why I felt I had to go there that night, but I did. It was almost as if the car was driving itself.

✢ ✡ ✢

When I walked into the room with the red walls, adrenaline-infused blood engorged my veins. Would I fight or flee? And if I fought, what dark power was I up against? I saw Jared reclining on a black leather couch. He looked like Jesus in a Pietà, draped languidly there. His head, with the small growth of beard, was thrown back, and one arm was draped over the top of the sofa as if it were a woman. His long legs were crossed at the ankle. Candles burned around him. Thick white wax in sconces, dripping rivulets.

I stood in the doorway like a stunned beast as I watched William approach from the other side of the room. He wore a black suit and a white shirt. His hands and face glowed in the darkness with that preternatural pallor. He turned his head slowly to look at me.

"Char. You've come to our party? I wasn't expecting you." So calm. His mouth was curved into an almost-smile. Dark eyes. They feed you with their eyes. Like black milk.

"Jared," I said, "I want you to get up now. Come with me."

Jared moved his head, but the rest of his body stayed reclined, perfectly motionless, like the statue he resembled. He blinked at me, and I took that as a good sign, that blink. He was still in there.

"Jared, I want you to come with me." I tried to make it sound light. "We have a date, remember? It's going to be all right."

On the walls of the room were mounted glass boxes with crumbling vampire bats inside of them. Children might have been afraid. To me, they looked even more pathetic than when William put them there years ago.

"Charlotte Emerson. This is between me and Jared. He found me. This is what he wants. Please leave."

"Jared . . ." I walked closer to him.

His eyes were pleading with me. He wanted it so badly. He wanted it more than he wanted me. I could see that. I thought I'd brought back his desire to live, but it wasn't enough. He wanted to live forever. There was nothing I could do.

Then we heard footsteps, and we all turned and a girl was standing in the room with us. A girl with brown ringlets and big dark eyes. She was dressed in a tight red dress that showed off her breasts and tiny hips. High red satin shoes on her feet. Her nails were painted red, too, and her lips. I even thought I recognized the shade. M.A.C. Viva Glam. Her skin was bone-china white.

She went up to William Stone Eliot, and he put his arm around her. He was so much bigger that his hand dangled over her breast. My spine convulsed with chills.

"So, here she is," she said.

"Emily? What . . ."

"I was wondering when you'd show up. I should hate you, but I don't. Because now I get everything you had and you have nothing except guilt."

I rushed forward and grabbed Jared's hand. He had

turned almost as white as the girl. He was sobbing.

I dragged him out of the room before he knew what I was doing. I put him in my Porsche. His eyes rolled up in his head.

"She is back," he said, before he passed out cold on the black leather.

Psychography

My hands were shaking. Never before, since my human existence, had my hands shaken. They were always still, and steady as marble. I gripped the steering wheel and rounded the curves of the Pacific Coast Highway. When I arrived at my house, Jared was still passed out. I got out of the car and hauled him up the front steps. I was not used to feeling weakness in my limbs; it frightened me.

I heaved Jared down onto the couch in the front room, almost falling on top of him. My hands were so unsteady I could hardly light the candles or pour the wine. The shaking in my hands seemed to be telling me something. There was something I must do.

I sat at the table with the red cloth, the white wax from the candles pooling onto it, and picked up the pen. After William changed me, I did not believe I could write any more poetry, anything at all. I was too empty. Writing poetry seemed to be another aspect of the human world lost, like crying, giving birth, producing milk or dying. I remembered how I practiced psychography, a way to communicate with the spirits, to feel less alone after Charles died. Loneliness was one thing William had not taken away. In fact, he had bestowed it upon me to a chilling degree.

Now my fingers tapped on the paper before me. There was an ache in my fingertips, all the nerve endings pricking like pins. This also reminded me of something from a distant past, a time when I felt an almost painful desire to write my feelings down on paper. I was changing; I wanted to understand what had happened to Emily and I had no idea where else to begin, so I picked up the pen.

my darling in the red dress

you would never have worn red in the past, not even a dress unless i gave it to you, not that one.

do you know that in the beginning there was a disease that drained all the fluids from the body, made the skin of the face look masklike, made the teeth appear to grow longer from the shrunken gums? did you know that this, my dear, is, as the great bard would say (perhaps he, too, was one of us and lives on somewhere in hiding), our parent, our original? perhaps we are not even real, we are only the demons made up by humans to explain a kind of death they did not understand or a way to frighten their children into being good or just the product of an artist's capricious mind.

perhaps we are only a psychosis.

my darling, was that you standing in william stone eliot's room in the red dress, looking more beautiful and also more vile than any girl i have ever seen? your jared couldn't look away.

your jared, but is he? or is he now mine? at least he was for a moment before your fearsome return.

the night bows down to you; the fires sweep the hills like torn remnants of your dress; the scent of night-blooming jasmine, pittosporum and chlorine from the pool we swam in is obliterated by the singed smell.

when i see us swimming in that pool, i see something else. i see william hiding in the bushes, watching us and listening to the words we speak.

"on nights like this, when everything's so beautiful, i want to live forever."

emily, who did this to you? did he come

back all this way for this alone? i thought he
came for me at first, but now i see.

   he came for you.

   or did he?

   and where was i? what actions did i take?
that night, that night you left this world.

   or did you? did you rise again?

   who did this to you, emily, who who who?

   and if it was not william eliot, then i must
understand more than who.

   i must know how and why.

The Exchange

I was slumped at the table, with my head in my arms, when Jared shook me awake the next evening. We had both slept straight through.

His eyes looked red and swollen, and his cheeks were bloated and bloodless. His big hand gripped my shoulder.

"What did you do?" he shouted.

"What?" Everything was a blur. I remembered a red room with writing on the walls. Jared lying on a couch, like a statue of Jesus. That infernal candlelight, and a girl in a red dress.

"I wanted to become like you!" he screamed. "That's all I wanted. I finally had my chance. It wouldn't have been on your head at all. I found him and he agreed, and you ruined it."

"Why, Jared? Why did you want to be like me? So that you could be with Emily again? Did you know about her all along?"

He staggered back as if I had bitten him. "What the hell are you talking about? What about Emily?"

"She was there. In the red dress. You saw her. She's one now."

"I didn't.... That was a dream. You saw my dream. That wasn't . . ."

And then, before he could say another word, the Santa Anas blew the window open, the frame slamming the wall. Two figures were in the room. They had brought the night with them.

Emily had changed out of her red dress. She wore a long, black lace sleeveless gown with a deep neckline.

The hemline fell to the ground, and under it, through the sheer fabric, you could see she had on black riding boots. William stood behind her with his hand on her shoulder.

She looked into my eyes, so deep into the dark, bloody depths of who I was, and I knew that this was not a dream and that none of this would be happening if I had not done something, something as shocking and evil as anything William Stone Eliot had ever done.

Someone had made Emily into a vampire. Someone had made me into a human. I did not understand it all yet, but I knew I was somehow to blame for what had occurred.

"Forgive me," I said.

"There is nothing to forgive," said Emily. "I have what I always wanted. Except for one thing."

William stepped closer, "Now give us Jared, please."

Emily was staring at Jared. She was wrapping

her curls around her index fingers, pulling, then letting them bounce back. She had a sly, kittenish expression on her lips. Jared stood behind me. I could feel the fear coming off his body like dry ice.

"Emily," he finally whispered, stepping forward.

"She's not Emily, Jared." I turned to face him.

"Oh, really! And who are you, then?" Emily asked. "What happened to the girl you used to be when Billy changed you?"

"She's not herself anymore," I said to Jared, ignoring her.

"What am I, then? A monster? That's funny. A monster calling the monster a monster!" Emily started to laugh.

Jared looked at me pleadingly. "What happened?" he asked me. There were tears in his eyes. "Tell me what happened! Who did this to her? Was it him? Did he kill her and bring her back? Did I bring her back because I wanted her so much?"

"I'll tell you," William answered, stepping between me and Jared. "Charlotte killed your Emily. Or almost killed her. I came along just in time. I saw that pretty face, those sweet eyes and lips. I knew I couldn't live without her, and I heard her ask for it. 'On nights like this, when everything is so beautiful, I want to live forever.'"

The room seemed to be growing smaller. "What did you say?" I grabbed William's arm, but he brushed me away like an insect.

"So I made her," he said. "But it was almost too late. Too much damage had been done. I had to make a bargain, an exchange."

"What are you talking about?" I lunged at him, and he caught me in his arms. "That thing you said! About Emily wanting to live forever. You heard her say that? She said that to me."

"Yes, darling. I was watching it all."

"You were there? How dare you! You have always tried to control me. Always!"

William smiled. "Perhaps. But look what you have received now. Look what I have given you."

And he touched a finger to my cheek, wet it in my tears, and dabbed the salty substance onto his lips.

Rage

That night Emily had brought her boyfriend, Jared Pierce, over to my house. They'd already been drinking when they arrived and stood swaying on my doorstep, giggling, a bottle of red wine in Emily's hands.

I remember thinking, *You are so lucky, Emily. You are both so lucky.*

She didn't need to bother with makeup or pretty clothes. He loved her in a baggy sweatshirt, cutoffs and sneakers. She barely came up to his armpit. He was so tall that even I felt small next to him, almost petite. I loved that feeling.

"Can we go swimming in your pool, Char?" Emily cooed. "Please?"

I let them in and we drank the wine and ate some caviar.

"Ooh, salty fish eggs, yum," Emily said. At that moment she sounded childish to me in an affected way, not like her lovely, innocent self. Jared didn't say much at all, but I could feel him watching me, and I could tell Emily noticed. Her eyes flicked back and forth between us like black butterflies.

"You're *so* dressed up!" she said in a hard little voice full of italics. "I don't think I've *ever* seen you without makeup and jewelry. It's *so* grown-up of you."

Jared looked nervous, picking up on the female tension. It was hard to miss, more obvious than the huge antique-jade necklace I wore.

"Put on Interpol!" Emily squealed. She was taking off her baggy sweatshirt. Under it she had a boy's white undershirt and no bra—the usual. She ran outside. "It's cold! But the water's warm. Oh my God! Jared, come on!"

He followed her out there. He'd hardly said a word to me the whole time. I watched them strip. His body looked huge next to hers. He got in the pool and held her, and I knew that under the water she was wrapping her legs around his waist.

I came and stood by the pool. The garden lights streaked the water with pale, shaking light. I undressed slowly, expecting them to watch me, but Emily pulled Jared around so his back was to me, and she started kissing him. Neither of them saw my perfect white body, naked and glowing in the night like a rare flower that, if plucked and consumed, could bring eternal life. *They have no idea what they are missing*, I thought.

But the truth was, I was the one missing out. And I knew it.

I remembered that day by the lake so long ago, older than human memory. Monster memory, it was.

But I was not a monster yet. I was a girl as beautiful as a flowering tree, undressing for a boy as beautiful as a lake. And as much as I was a part of the trees and he was a part of the lake, we were even more a part of each other. I was a girl diving into the blue water, splashing and swimming and happy and never imagining that the boy would be taken from me and that I would have to grieve for eternity.

Then rage surged up in me. Rage at any god that would take my brother from me. Rage at the devil for using my grief as a trap to make me his. Rage at time, at history, at memory, at all humanity with its cruelty in the face of endless loss. And rage at this happy mortal boy and girl playing in the water, in my pool, with no fear, no loss, no sense that someday they would be without their beloved and that the someday would last for an eternity.

I don't remember what happened next, but I know that William Eliot was telling the truth when he revealed the terrible thing that I had done.

Suddenly, like a nightmare remembered hours later, one so brutal as to be only worse in the bright of day, it all came back to me.

i follow you home and wait outside your window.

i watch, seething and bucking with my rage while you and jared make love on your little-girl bed.

i wait until he leaves, and then i go inside and bend over your small, beckoning body.

"Charlotte," you say. Your voice is thick with alcohol and dreaming. "What are you doing here?"

I am so ashamed of what I am, in contrast to your innocence.

"I know what you are," you say.

I feel as if I've been struck in the chest with something sharp. Suddenly I wonder why I came here. What led me to your door as if under some spell. I pull away, full of remorse.

You go on. "I want to be what you are."

I have never made a human into what I am. I have never felt the desire, nor did I believe I would have the restraint not to go all the way and take a life in the process.

i am choked with a thirst i have never felt.

i lose all restraint, all sense of humanity.

i beome the beast, and i pierce the beauty, pierce your shallow wrists with your own pocket knife, and then i feed until you are dry.

or almost dry.

because that is when william, who has been watching me for days, who has followed me through the night, who has masterminded it all, swoops in and changes you while i stagger home alone and without a memory of what i have done.

you will be buried so no one will suspect, and then you will rise out of the crypt and walk with him.

and in those moments when william bargained for your soul, i had no idea that both our greatest wishes were being fulfilled, or at what great cost.

Meet the Monster

"Is it true, Char?" Jared was staring at Emily. "Tell me! Is it true? You did this?"

At first I couldn't answer him. I couldn't look at him. I turned to William.

"Why did you come back again?" I asked. "You said you wanted to release me. Why did you come to my house the other night?"

"I came to see if the bargain really worked."

"Emily!" Jared rushed at her and tried to grab her dress, but she moved back imperceptibly, and he fell to his knees on the carpet like the man in

Rodin's sculpture *Eternal Idol*.

"Who did this to you? Tell me! Is it true?"

I had to answer him. I had to look at him. My face was burning. "Yes, Jared. It was me. I am a monster. That is what monsters do," I said. There were so many tears pouring from my eyes that I couldn't see him. I tried to touch him, but he pushed my hand away.

"You never said that. You never said you killed anyone."

"I didn't remember until now." Now it was I who wanted to fall to my knees.

"You lied to me."

"No. Everything I said was the truth. Except one thing. I said I couldn't feel love, only desire. That was true with William and with Emily. But not with you. Something has changed."

"Yes, it has." William smiled. "She's changed, Jared. I exchanged her for Emily. She is a mortal just like you now. Do you want to stay like that, growing old and wrinkled and diseased, riddled with tumors, then rotting in your grave? Or do you want to come with me and your true love, Emily? I never minded male companionship. We'd have quite a time, the three of us. We'd rule the world."

He walked slowly over to where Jared remained kneeling on my carpet, covering his face with his hands. Then William stroked Jared's black hair, his jawline.

"Jared!" I screamed. "Don't let him! Think what you want about me. Do what you want to me. But don't go with them."

Emily looked at Jared, and he rose as if she had pulled him by invisible strings. He stood in front of her, staring at her face. Then he strode over to me. His hand slapped my cheek, so hard that I reeled around and crashed against a cabinet. The Ming vase fell from its alcove and shattered on the floor.

I crawled to Jared and grabbed at his ankles. "I will go away. I will never bother you again. But you must stay away from them! You must."

Jared turned away from me.

"Forgive me, Emily," I said, staggering to my feet. "Forgive me. You were my best friend. You suffered enough."

I saw Emily then, Emily as a girl, not as this monster, like the monster I had been for so long. She was asleep in her bed, and the door opened and a man stumbled in. His breath smelled of whiskey. His hands were huge and calloused. He was more of a monster than what she had become. And now I knew, looking at Emily and William, that the man, Emily's mother's ex-boyfriend, the one who had raped her, wherever he was, had not much time left to live.

I ran to the door and took the keys to my Porsche, and I left them there, the three I loved or had once loved or had thought I loved.

"Jared," I said from the doorway, "you brought me back to life."

He was looking at Emily again, but when I spoke I saw him turn, and for a moment I thought I recognized regret upon his face.

William shouted after me as I escaped into the night. "Wrong again, Charlotte. I am the one who made you alive. As you said, I am always the one."

Why
Billy Came Back

I drove around for a while, not knowing where to go, half wishing to smash into a wall or to go over an embankment. I was speeding on Sunset, tires screeching around the curves, when the vision hit me like a semi that had lost its brakes and swerved to the wrong side of the road.

In my mind I saw the club where I'd gone with Emily and then Jared. I saw the line of kids outside. I saw Jared standing with William and Emily. Jared looked dazed, and Emily held him up. William was watching them with sneering eyes. He was wearing a long, dark trench coat.

He knew no one would stop him. No one would search him. He'd get inside the club. In fact, they'd let him in first, invite him to the front of the line because he and his party looked so good in their black clothes, with their pretty faces. They could have been models. No one questioned models. They could get away with murder. I know from experience.

Billy and Emily would read about the event in the newspapers tomorrow. They would shake their heads. *What a shame. All those young people. So much privilege and beauty, and their whole lives ahead of them . . .*

Emily wouldn't question him. It would take her years to put together the puzzle of all the chaos. There was so much in the world, anyway. This was the first time William had the bomb. Usually he just attracted disaster to himself. Now he was getting bored, getting bolder. He wanted to be in the very center of the explosion, with his new love beside him, and walk away with her untouched. There would be so much light! So much sound! The bombings in London and Hiroshima both happened while he was there. They were all beautiful in their way. And the boy would be off their hands. He had no intention of sharing Emily with him. . . .

A car horn blared and I startled, as if waking from a nightmare. But it wasn't a dream. I had seen what was coming.

I called 911 and screamed at the operator. "There's a bomb! Zanzibar. In Santa Monica. You have to help. You have to do something."

I kept on like a race car driver in hell. All I could think about was Jared. And the nightmares of the ages. The Black Dahlia's severed body. The kimono-flower scars of Hiroshima. The man dead under the tractor at Woodstock. Kurt Cobain with a bullet in his head.

I had seen the look of trust on Jared's face, his blind eyes. He would have followed Billy and Emily anywhere that night. He would have walked straight down into Hades with them. What was Hades, anyway? It was the fires in the hills of Malibu. It was a bomb in a nightclub. It was everywhere.

By the time I got to the club, they were at the front of the line. I stopped the Porsche in the middle of the street and got out. Cars honked and tires shredded and sparked as I ran through traffic across the road. Jared glanced up. His eyes met mine, and for a moment he looked like he understood. He started to walk toward me, but William held up his hand and pushed him back.

I threw myself at William.

"Fuck you! Let him go."

A smile passed over William's face. "You think you can avert disaster? You, who are always there, at the scene of the crime?"

"It's you! You're the one. It's all you!"

"You have less power over me now than ever, Charlotte Emerson."

It wasn't true. I finally had what he had taken away. What made me more powerful than before.

I was a human again.

The bouncer came over and grabbed my upper arm. "What's the problem here?"

"There's a bomb! He has a bomb!"

They all stepped back, and I dragged Jared across the street and pushed him behind a car as the police drove up to the club and, still smiling, William took Emily's hand and walked inside.

Happily,
Not Ever, After

I live in a tiny room now. A claw-footed tub stands behind a screen. The walls are brick. The floor is scratched wood. I have hardly any furniture, hardly any decorative objects or clothes. I wear the same pair of jeans; one black dress and one pair of black boots for work. I sold my car. I do not miss all the beauty. I have had enough.

My life is peaceful, though. I go to work at a cosmetics counter every day. I put makeup on women's faces. I like to see how happy it makes them when I hold the mirror up. I tell them they are beautiful. And they buy the products I sell because they know I am not lying. I think they are all beautiful, just because they are human.

At night, on my way home from work, I walk to the grocery store on the corner and buy a loaf of bread, some cheese and chocolate, a bottle of red wine and, once a week, a bouquet of fresh flowers. No more rare meat or any animal flesh at all, although I think about it sometimes, especially sushi. I light candles and sit on a cushion on the floor and eat. After that I read or watch a DVD.

I like old silent films in black and white. *Nosferatu.* Why do they make him so hideous-looking? That is a lie. *The Cabinet of Dr. Caligari. La Passion et la Mort de Jeanne d'Arc.* "Are you a good angel or a dark angel?" the mad monks ask Joan with her big eyes, her huge, real tears that catch the light. Once I was a dark angel, and now I am not an angel at all.

Sometimes I write. I am writing the story of who I was because there is no real story of who I am. I don't have any friends, only acquaintances, because I am afraid that I may accidentally reveal my secret past if I let my guard down. The only person I share that past with is Jared. I email him the story of my life as I write it. He never responds, but I keep sending pages anyway. It is worth the risk to know that he may be reading them.

I think of Emily often. Of what I did to her. In my jealousy, my rage. Of what I was. I know that I will never be free of the guilt, not even when I die, but at least there will be that escape some day, that leaving, in itself a redemption.

What I do most is think of Jared.

> *my darling boy*
>
> *sometimes i see you driving in a car, driving across deserts, past pastures, along coasts, through forests.*

i see you drinking coffee and eating burgers at roadside diners.

i see you sleeping in hotel rooms with peeling wallpaper, your long body spread out under pilling blankets and polyester bedspreads.

i don't know where you are going.

i can't see your eyes.

i can't feel your heart.

i don't know if you are still you.

or if you have become something else.

and i wait and i wait and i wait and i wait to know.

One night I finish my dinner and curl up in bed with a book when there is a knock on my door. Usually you have to be buzzed in; someone has gotten upstairs without that. I creep to the door and peep out.

Jared Pierce stands in the hallway. My heart wants to jump into his arms like a puppy, like a child.

I open the door and let him in without thinking.

He could kill me. He could be like William now. Like Emily. I don't care. I want to see him.

He looks thin and pale; his cheekbones are gaunt, his eyes red and swollen. He shivers in his black leather jacket. Southern California boys don't know about real winter coats. At least he wears his biker boots and black knit gloves and hat. How I want to make him warm.

"Come in and curl up by the radiator," I say.

"Charlotte . . ."

"Come in. I am always waiting for you."

He walks in slowly, stomping his feet as if to bring life back into numb toes. I am relieved at his discomfort; it means he has not been changed, is not impervious to the chill or to human emotion. I try to sniff him, to detect his human scent, but it's too cold.

We sit together on the floor. He eyes my bed warily, so I don't invite him there. He takes off his cap and stretches it in his hands.

"I read everything you sent me. I didn't know how to respond."

"You don't have to. I just wanted to send it to you. It's for you."

"Thank you."

He looks into my eyes so deeply I feel it in my stomach.

"I'm so sorry, Jared. Please forgive me."

"No, I'm sorry. For hitting you."

"I deserved it. I was a monster."

He takes my face gently in his hands and makes me look at him. "Did you really kill her?"

I start to cry and choke out the words. "I didn't know I did it. I've gone over and over it in my head. It was as if William orchestrated it somehow. He admitted he was watching me. He saw me with Emily and wanted her, and wanted to let me go. Do you believe me?"

He is silent for a moment. "I believe you. I saw what William is like, And I know you, Charlotte."

"I am a monster. Or I was."

"You saved my life. And you've changed, haven't

you? He was telling the truth?" His voice is anxious, almost pleading, praying it's true.

"Yes. I've changed. "

I see the relief on his face.

"You are part of the reason I changed, though, not just him. He can't control me anymore."

Jared bends his head so his black hair falls into his eyes. He takes off his gloves and I see that his knuckles are red and raw. I want to hold his hands, feel the pulse of mortal blood in his veins.

"Why did you go to William at all?" I hadn't meant to ask him this; it just came out. I sounded pathetic. "After our nights together."

"Those nights were the reason. I wanted to be with you forever. I loved Emily when we were together, but in a different way than I love you, Charlotte. And she was gone then. I thought he'd help me, since you wouldn't. I didn't understand that you weren't immortal anymore."

"And now that you know I'm not and Emily is . . . ?"

Jared puts his hand over my mouth. My lips against his fingers.

"After the explosion and you leaving, it was like I woke up. I saw what she had become and that you weren't what I thought. I knew I didn't want immortality. I only wanted you."

"But don't you wonder? Don't you still . . . ?"

"I love you, crazy," Jared answers softly. "I want to be with you now here, for as long as we have."

He takes my hands in his. I cannot smell his human scent or hear his blood or see color around his head. I no longer thirst for what runs through his veins or the clock in his chest with its limited beats. But now I can see. I close my eyes, and all I see inside his mind is a girl with shoulder-length dirty-blond hair, which splits at the ends when she does not trim it, and imperfect skin. It takes me a moment to recognize that she is me. She is about to turn eighteen.

And then Jared Dorian Pierce kisses Charlotte Emerson by the hissing radiator in the damaged city far from the one he had left behind, and I know that she is me and that somehow love, like a lost twin, like mortality, like the hope that our planet will survive long after we are gone, has been returned to us.

Francesca Lia Block, winner of the prestigious Margaret A. Edwards Award, is the author of many acclaimed and bestselling books, including WEETZIE BAT, DANGEROUS ANGELS: *The Weetzie Bat Books*, the collection of stories BLOOD ROSES, the poetry collection HOW TO (UN)CAGE A GIRL, and, most recently, the novel THE WATERS & THE WILD. Her work is published around the world. You can visit her online at www.francescaliablock.com.